CALIFORNIA CONNECTION

CALIFORNIA CONNECTION

CHUNICHI

www.urbanbooks.net

Urban Books
1199 Straight Path
West Babylon, NY 11704

ISBN- 13: 978-1-60162-075-0
ISBN- 10: 1-60162-075-6

First Printing December 2008
Printed in the United States of America

10 9 8 7 6 5 4 3

*This is a work of fiction. Any references or similarities to actual events, real
people, living, or dead, or to real locales are intended to give the novel a
sense of reality. Any similarity in other names, characters, places, and inci-
dents is entirely coincidental.*

Distributed by Kensington Publishing Corp.
Submit Wholesale Orders to:
Kensington Publishing Corp.
C/O Penguin Group (USA) Inc.
Attention: Order Processing
405 Murray Hill Parkway
East Rutherford, NJ 07073-2316
Phone: 1-800-526-0275
Fax: 1-800-227-9604

Prologue

California Jewel—Who in hell would name their child some shit like that? That's the first question that comes to mind when someone hears my name. Jewel, the name I actually went by, was given to me by my grandmother. She said I was more precious to her than a priceless stone. Now, California, that shit came from my whore-ass momma. She named me California because I was the product of a one-night stand she had in California.

Although I hated the name, as reckless as it seems, I be damned if any other name was more appropriate. California described me perfectly. Just like the state of California, I was full of sunshine. My pussy was wetter than a ripe California orange. I was definitely Hollywood when it came to my divalicious attitude, wanting what I want when I want it. But if you ever tried to cross me, I'd become more dangerous than the LAPD. To say the least, I was off the Richter, like a California earthquake knows exactly what I mean.

As if my flawless five-foot four-inch frame wasn't enough,

I just had partnered up with a beast by the name of Michael Burroughs. He was Mike to his family and baby mothers, but to cats getting money on the streets, he was known as Calico, short for "California Connection." And every nigga in the drug game dreamed of having a person like him on his side.

I, on the other hand, had made a different kind of connection with him, but little did I know just how far that connection would take me.

Chapter 1

"A Drunk Person Speaks a Sober Mind"

Jewel

"Fuck you, bitch!" I held up my middle finger as I grabbed my oversized Chanel bag then stormed out of my now ex-manager's office. "And take this and shove it up your big, white, cottage cheese ass," I said to the overweight, unattractive wench that had just fired me. I knocked over the carnation flower arrangement that sat in the waiting area of the medical office then slung a few magazines across the floor on my way out the door.

Thinking of how that wicked witch had just tried to humiliate me, I just wasn't quite satisfied with my tantrum, so I stopped in front of the huge window that covered the entire front of the office and pulled down my pants. "Oh, and you all can kiss my big, plump, juicy ass!" I yelled as I smacked my butt cheeks then ran off laughing.

Now my heart was content, and I was able to get in my truck at ease. *That bitch had some nerve calling me out in front of the entire staff and patients, making it seem like I was some sort of incompetent young black chick.* I started up my white

Range Rover, the words *DATBICH* on my license plate, a message to let everyone know who was driving this here whip, and zoomed out of the parking lot, leaving nothing but dust.

Evidently that chick didn't read between the lines of my resume. Of course, I had plenty of medical billing experience, but I also was first a born hustler that could game any nigga, and second a ghost writer, which translated to, "I'm not dependent solely on your fucking pissy-ass check, bitch!" That working shit was never for a chick like me anyway.

If it wasn't for my homeboy Touch, I would have never been working in the first place. His words were still fresh in my head as I pulled out the parking lot and onto the busy street. "Keep you a lil' gig on the side, Jewel," he'd say. This nigga insisted that I should always keep a plan B, no matter how much loot I had coming in. I enjoyed having the extra cash on hand, but I didn't know if that advice was for my benefit or his. I think that was simply a way to keep me out of his pockets.

Touch was my boy, so if I were to ever fall on hard times, he would've definitely come through for me, but he knew that I liked keeping my pockets swollen. Regardless, I was on my grind and had money coming in from every direction. My new career as a ghostwriter was really taking off, and I always had a nigga or two that I was constantly gaming. Hell, that's how I was able to afford my whip and my crib. Me getting fired from that job was actually a blessing in disguise. Now there would be less stress, and more time to focus on my writing, the real money-maker.

I connected my iPod to the radio and blasted the tune "Glamorous" by Fergie as I headed to the bank to deposit my check. I thought about my manager on the way. *That bitch didn't know I was already living the fucking glamorous life.*

She ain't doing no damage here. I laughed as I pulled up to the bank's drive-thru.

From the bank, I headed to the nail shop. I began to laugh again as I thought about what was happening. *How many people get fired from their job then go get their nails done? Only a real fucking diva like myself.*

I had to call my girl Sasha and let her in on my drama for the day. I smiled as I scrolled to her name in contacts and the picture of her from the back, wearing only a thong, with a whip thrown over her shoulder, popped up on the screen of my iPhone. Sasha was my girl. Although we'd only been friends a couple of years and we'd met on some strange terms at the strip club, she was still on a different level than any of my other friends. She and I had a little closer connection, a connection that I shared with her only.

I waited patiently for Sasha to pick up as I sang along to the reggae tune "Can't Breathe" by Tanya Stephens, which she had set as her call tone. You can always tell what a bitch was going through by her call tone or voice mail.

"Hello?" Sasha answered right away.

"What's up, Boobie?" I called her by her pet name. "I gotta tell you about my day at work."

"Oh Lord! What the hell that fat bitch done this time?" Sasha was aware of the daily drama I had with my stupid-ass manager.

"Bitch, why that fat cow fire me?"

"For real, girl?" Sasha asked in disbelief.

"Yes, bitch. She gon' come at me with some bullshit about the collections versus production is showing a huge gap"—My sentence was disrupted by the sight of a fine-ass nigga passing by in a black drop-top 2008 Mercedes Benz SL550 that screamed, "I'm that nigga!" My eyes were glued to him as he passed by slowly. I saw nothing but his cornrows, dark chocolate skin, ice grill, at least a three karat diamond stud in his right ear, as he chatted away on his cell phone. It was as though everything was moving in slow motion. I gave him my most seductive look, and he glanced at me from the corner of his eye.

"Jewel! Jewel!"

"Oh shit. Sorry about that baby. I just saw this fine-ass dude, umph!"

I felt a shiver in my pussy as I thought about what I could do with a guy like him on my team. He could possibly take the place of my MVP and turn him to a bench-rider. His looks were one thing, but his money was what really made my pussy wet. And after getting fired, I was definitely in search for a new player on the team to compensate for my lost wages.

I'd learned the rules to gaming a dude at a very young age. I'd watched my mom use and abuse men my entire life. Her father had left her at a young age, and it seemed liked she was never able to get past it. At a very young age my mother taught me to trust no man, never wear my heart on my sleeve, and to always stand my ground, because kindness was a sign of weakness. A while later she taught me the power of beauty and the booty.

As an adult, I'd fallen right into my mother's footsteps. I guess it's true what they say, the apple doesn't fall too far from the tree, because I'd mastered the art of gold-digging, just as she did. It was like a gift. I could look at a guy and assess him in a matter of seconds and know approximately how much dough he was holding, and where it came from. In my book, looks alone didn't get a man anywhere, but money would get him everywhere. Don't get it twisted though, this book I'm referring to isn't titled, *The Whore Handbook*. It's more like *The Gold-digger's Guide to Financial Security*.

* * *

"Girl, you crazy. You ain't never gon' change," Sasha said in a disapproving tone.

"Why you sound like that? Did I say something wrong?"

I could tell by the tone of Sasha's voice that something was bothering her. It was a tone I was way too familiar with. I just didn't know whether it was something I said, or if it was a personal struggle.

When we'd first met, her life was going downhill, but we pulled together to turn things around. Sasha started off stripping at Blue Light in Hampton, a city about thirty minutes from Virginia Beach, and life was good for her. She had a house she lived in, a townhouse that she rented out to Section 8 recipients, and a nice car. She needed for nothing. But when she stabbed a chick during an altercation, she was fired from the club, and her world began to crumble. Sasha decided that the strip scene was no longer for her, and wanted to work.

Although she had little work experience and education, I was still able to put something together for her. Luckily, she'd actually gone to school for medical assistance and worked in a couple of medical offices. But during her time as a successful dancer, she figured she would never see this kind of money working a regular job, so she let her certification expire. Even though odds were against us, I created an exaggerated, yet professional resume and cover letter for her, and used some of my connections in the medical field to land her a job with Sentara Healthcare.

At first, everything was smooth sailing, more or less, but it didn't last long. Nearly a year later it had almost become routine for Sasha to call me with some depressing news. It was as though someone had put a curse on her ass or something. In six months alone she'd gotten in trouble with the authorities for welfare fraud. Then she lost her investment property, and as if things couldn't possibly get any worse, her baby father got robbed.

"I can't take this stress anymore," Sasha said, bursting into tears.

"What stress, baby?" I asked, wanting to know what was bothering my friend.

"It's like everything is going so wrong so fast. I'm working my ass off, but with my monthly bills, plus the money for daycare and gas, it's just not worth it. I can't keep living like this, Jewel."

"So what you want to do?"

"I don't know. I guess I'm gonna have to start back dancing. I've got to get these bills caught up. Since Rick got robbed, he ain't been able to help out, and I'm at risk of losing everything I own. I'm gonna lose my house."

Now my first instinct was to tell her about that deadbeat-ass baby father of hers. There ain't no way a broke-down dude would be living up in my shit and can't even pay a light bill. Who gives a fuck if he got robbed? That's part of the fucking game, and a real hustler always knows how to get back on.

Besides, where the fuck was his stash? I didn't even bother going into that with Sasha because I'd heard all the excuses once before—"He decided to get out of the game since he got robbed. He's trying to start his own business." Trying to stay focused on Sasha's needs instead of her downfalls, I directed my attention back to her statement.

"So how you gonna do that, Sasha?" I knew that once you got a bad rep in the stripping world in this area, your career was basically over. "I thought you were blackballed on the whole dance scene in this area?"

"Well, I heard girls be going to Atlanta and New York

and be racking up. Maybe I could just go to Atlanta for a couple of weeks and then come back and hit New York on the weekends. All I need is money to get my business licenses and plane ticket. Plus, my mom lives in Columbus, Georgia. That's only an hour away from Atlanta. I could take the boys there to stay with her until I get on my feet, and I could crash at her crib the weeks I'm there dancing. What you think?"

I knew Sasha wasn't so much asking me what I thought of her idea, but moreso what I thought about giving her the money to carry it out.

"Hey, I've always supported your decision. If you think this is what's best. So I take it you're gonna quit your job?" I asked, since she so conveniently forgot to mention her job when explaining her master plan.

"I have to. I mean, I have no other choice. I need fast money, Jewel. They 'bout to foreclose on my house."

"A'ight, Sasha," I said, disappointed in my her actions. We'd gone through a lot to get her that job, and now she was leaving it to go right back where she started. "How much you need for the business license and plane ticket?"

Almost before I could finish my sentence, she quickly responded, "Like six hundred."

"Okay. I'll call you later, and you can come get it."

"Thank you so much. I promise I'll pay you back," Sasha said, full of excitement.

"Yeah, Sasha. I'm 'bout to get my nails done. I'll hit you later."

I wrapped up the call knowing damn well I would never see that six hundred dollars again. I'd lost count of the number of times I'd lent her money and never saw it again, so I never held my breath on a promise to pay. That was always a promise waiting to be broken.

"Love you," she sang into the phone.

"Love you too, Boobie." I disconnected the call and jumped out the truck and headed for the nail shop.

"Hey, Kim," I said to my nail tech as I walked in the nail shop.

She said, "Me not Kim. Me tell you every time."

And she was right. She did tell me every time, but I always managed to forget, until she reminded me.

"I want a manicure, pedicure, eyebrow wax, upper lip wax, and eyelashes," I said, running off my list.

"Sit here," she said, directing me to the spa pedicure chair. Then she asked about my homeboy, Touch, who regularly came to the nail shop with me. "Where ya friend?"

"Good question." I turned on the chair's massager then pulled out my cell phone to give him a call.

I relaxed as I waited for him to answer. Boy, was I drained. I didn't know if it was just the events from the day or Sasha's constant issues that drained me, but whichever it was, it was nothing a little pampering couldn't solve.

"You have reached the voice mail box of . . ." the recording began to say, letting me know that Touch wasn't available.

Maybe to the average chick or someone else he wasn't available, but he was always available for me, so I dialed his other cell phone number.

Touch was like my brother. We'd been friends since high school. When I'd first moved to Virginia Beach from Compton, California, all the chicks were hating on me, and all the dudes were loving me. But it didn't take long for me to sort out the real gangsters from the fake ones, and when it was all said and done, there was only a couple left standing. One, Diablo James, I made my high school sweetheart, and Touch, the other, I made my best friend. We clicked immediately.

As a native Southerner, I was used to seeing many black

people and few white people. Sure, segregation was over, but deep in the South, black people stuck together, and the white people did the same. You might call it voluntary segregation—They didn't bother us, and we didn't bother them. So when I came to Virginia Beach, it was way too many white people, and way too many black people that acted white for me. For me, it was like moving from Compton to the Valley.

Touch, coming straight from the streets of Norfolk to the center of Virginia Beach, experienced the same culture shock as me. He felt my pain. It was like we were in the fucking twilight zone. So being the natural rebels we were, we acted out and did our own gotdamn thang.

A born hustler, Trayvon Davis knew how to get money by any means. People said that everything he touched turned to gold, so he was given the name Touch by the streets. Unlike most dope boys, Touch had never experienced a loss, never had a nigga buck on him, and never had weak product. He'd been dealt the best of hands in this here poker game of the streets.

Touch's parents moved their family to Virginia Beach during his high school years to keep him out of trouble, but with my help, he was able to get back and forth to Norfolk on a daily basis. But he couldn't stay out of trouble at all, which was why he ultimately got sent to the penitentiary.

My homeboy spent three long years of his life locked up. But since he got out, shit had been nothing but uphill for him. Keeping the truth to his name, he was still turning shitballs to gold nuggets.

"What up, bay?" Touch answered right away.

"Nothing. I'm at the nail shop. Meet me here. I need some company. Then afterwards we can go have some drinks." Drinking wasn't my thing, but Touch's borderline alcoholic ass loved it.

"A'ight. I'll be up there." He already knew I was at our regular spot, which was just around the corner from his crib.

"Hey, sexy," I said to Touch as he walked in.

Never the flashy type but always dressed tight, Touch demanded attention as he entered a room. He always wore the latest styles but never any jewelry. You could catch him with a different color Prada or latest Gucci sneaker on each day of the week, but you won't catch him with an iced-out chain. The most he would have on was a watch. He didn't even have his ears pierced. No jewels, not even a tattoo, he was the most humble nigga around, with enough charisma to charm anyone. Touch managed to get any bitch he wanted. Now, how many niggas would love to be in his shoes?

Before Touch had a chance to respond to my sexy comment, another nail technician directed him to sit beside me. "You can sit here."

Touch sat down and slid off his Gucci slippers and rolled up his Antik Denim jeans to prepare for his pedicure then focused his attention to me. He looked at me with his thick cornrows and with those big brown eyes as another nail tech grabbed his hand to begin his manicure.

"What's up, homie?"

"I got fired today." I laughed.

"Stop playing," Touch said in disbelief.

"Yep."

"You a'ight?" he asked.

"Hell yeah. You know I didn't want to work anyway."

"So you gonna look for another job?"

"I have a job, damn it!" I yelled.

"A'ight, a'ight," Touch said quickly.

"And answer your damn phone." I said, acknowledging his phone that had been ringing constantly since we began our conversation. "I'm sick of hearing that shit ring."

"It's my baby mother. She on some bullshit right now, and I ain't into that arguing shit."

"Your baby mother is a trip." I grinned as I thought back to the many stories I'd heard about her. "What you do now, Touch?" I asked, automatically assuming it was his fault.

"I ain't did shit. She just pissed about my new girl. They stay into it. My baby mother be calling her phone and all kinds of shit."

I couldn't do nothing but laugh as Touch continued to tell me about his baby momma drama. Normally, I would be the first bitch to snap when he would tell me about a chick doing him wrong, but when it came to his baby mother, it was nothing but love. I had to respect her because she was just so gangster with her shit. Real talk, she reminded me of myself. Everything she did was some shit I would do.

I feel sorry for the nigga that ever decided to make me his baby mother. A nigga better marry me because, trust me, the shit I would do if my baby father left me would make them give baby momma drama a whole new name.

"It's okay, pookie face. We'll go drink our problems away in a few minutes." I reached over and rubbed the side of his face, careful not to smear my freshly painted nails.

Sticking her little-ass nose all up in my business, the one I called Kim said, "You like him. He not friend. He boyfriend."

"What?" I balled my face up.

"You like him." She pointed to Touch.

"Go 'head wit' dat shit," Touch told her. "Dis my fucking sista."

Although I was pissed that bitch was all in my business, I knew where she was coming from. It wasn't the first time somebody had said that same shit. Hell, all of our friends swore we were fucking. Anybody on the outside looking in felt it was a little more than a tight friendship between us. As crazy as it may seem, they were all wrong. Touch and I hadn't even held hands before, let alone kiss. That nigga was truly my best friend, nothing more, nothing less.

"Yo," Touch answered his other cell phone as I headed to the back of the nail shop to get my waxing done.

"Don't make my eyebrows too thin," I instructed as I lay on the bench to wait for my wax.

"It not too thin," the nail technician tried explaining in her best English. "I do nice for you."

"Okay. I hope so, 'cause last week you made them way too thin."

As a mixed breed, Panamanian and black, my eyebrows were naturally thick, so thin eyebrows did me no justice. A full face, a head full of thick, curly hair, and little skinny eyebrows wasn't the business.

"Shit!" I yelled as the nail tech ripped the tape from beneath my eyebrow.

I knew getting wax was no piece a cake, but I didn't ever remember it being that painful. For a moment I thought that little Vietnamese bitch was applying a little extra force on some get-back shit.

Ten minutes later my waxing was complete. I looked in the mirror closely to examine the wax job I'd just received. Surprisingly, it was perfect.

"It looks good. Can you do it like this next week too?" I asked as I handed back the little woman the hand mirror.

"I told you, I do nice job for you," she responded as she headed out the door, and I followed her to the cash register.

Touch sat in a chair near the register. "You done, yo?"

"Yep."

"Let's roll." Touch pulled off four twenties from a stack of money he carried in his pocket and paid for our services.

"Keep the change," I said, as though I'd just paid the eighty dollars for our day at the nail shop.

"See, me told you he your boyfriend," Kim said, as Touch and I walked out the door.

"Whatever," I said, choosing to no longer entertain her foolishness. "See you next week." I asked Touch as we walked to our vehicles. "Where we headed?"

"I thought we was gon' get a drink?"

"Said like a true alcoholic," I said, noticing the panic in Touch's voice. He was like a fiend needing his daily fix. "We are going to get a drink, hon. I was just asking where."

"Oh shit. Let's hit the beach," Touch said, now much more relaxed.

"You want me to jump in with you, or should I drive?" I asked, knowing Touch's tendency to want to stay at the bar longer than me.

I couldn't count the number of times I'd left him at the bar alone. And the funny shit was that no one would ever know he was there alone. Being the social type and loving white people, he had no problems mingling and fitting right in at the bars on the oceanfront. You would think they would single out a young black dude with cornrows from Norfolk. But, I guess, when you got something they all wanted, they wouldn't care if you dressed like André 3000, had hair like Bob Marley, and spoke like Ozzy Osbourne.

Touch was a real businessman, and knew how to pick his clients, suppliers, and workers. On top of all that, this nigga was just so fucking reserved, never the greedy type. Although it rarely showed, Touch also had a dark side that would come out and show its dirty little head when a nigga got out of line. Even with all that, he still didn't think like the average dope boy. He had bigger goals like businesses, houses, investments, and setting up college funds for his twin daughters, his pride and joy.

"Go 'head and drive, 'cause I gotta meet my man there and I don't know how long this nigga gon' take."

"Okay, lead the way." I pressed the unlock button on my keychain and headed to my truck.

I knew exactly what it meant when Touch said he had to

meet his man. Touch tried his hardest to exclude me from his dealings with the drug game, but I knew him way too well. Although I can honestly say I'd never saw a drug transaction go down or even seen the product, as a matter of fact, I still knew what was up. Of course, Touch had legit businesses, but I still knew he had his ties with the game, quiet as it was kept. I'd have been a fool to think otherwise.

I hopped in the truck and grabbed my iPod and set it to some riding music. I could kiss the muthafucka that invented that shit. The radio was nearly nonexistent in my world. No time for a bunch of commercials and constantly changing the station, trying to find a song I enjoy. Then when it came to CD's, I hated shuffling through a big-ass CD case and loading and unloading CD's into the deck. My heart goes out to those still living in those prehistoric ways.

Not even ten whole minutes had passed before we reached Atlantic Avenue at the oceanfront, better known as "the strip." I pulled into the beach parking lot behind Touch as he paid for the both of us. By the time I was parked and getting out of my truck, he was already headed to the bar.

I yelled at Touch across the parking lot, "Gotdamn, you fucking wino! Slow down. They ain't gonna run out of liquor before you get there."

Touch waited for me at the door of the bar and held the door open for me to walk in. "Do you have to be so damn loud? You used to be a little prissy-ass beach girl; now you ghetto as fuck!"

I paused in the doorway and looked him in the eyes. "I'm prissy when the time calls for it, and I'm ghetto when the time calls for that," I said and proceeded to walk past.

Touch smacked my ass as he followed me in the bar. "Whatever, nigga."

"Ugh! Don't ever touch my booty," I said, surprised at Touch's actions.

"You just started getting an ass. Back in high school, you were straight up and down, *miss nasatall.*" Touch joked as we grabbed a seat at the bar.

"Oh, I know you didn't. You trying to say I had *no ass at all.*" I laughed at Touch's taunting.

Our conversation was interrupted by Touch's incoming call.

"Yo."

I could hear the person ask from the other end of the phone, "Where you at?"

"The front," Touch said, trying to give his location without actually saying the words.

Niggas kill me with that shit. They act like every phone is tapped and every phone call is being recorded by the damn feds. I grinned to myself as he continued his conversation.

The overly tanned white woman with obvious breast implants laid napkins in front of Touch and me. "What cha having to drink?"

I ordered Touch's usual. "X-Rated and Sprite for me, and Grey Goose on the rocks for him."

After ending his call, Touch asked, "You ordered for me?"

"Yeah," I lied. "I got you a Hennessy and Coke."

"What? Why the fuck you do that, Jewel?"

I continued to lie just to see how aggravated Touch would get. "I thought that's what you drink?"

"Man." Touch sucked his teeth and called for the bartender. "Yo!"

The bartender put up one finger as she made our drinks, signaling that she would be right over in a moment.

"You goin' to drink that fucking Hennessy too." Touch pulled out a cigarette.

I didn't even respond as I watched the bartender bring our drinks over and sit them directly in front of us.

"What can I get for you, hon?" she asked Touch.

"Man, let me get a Grey Goose on the rocks," he ordered, not even noticing the drink sitting right in front of him.

"Another one?" the bartender asked.

Touch looked down and grinned. "Nah, this good," he said to the bartender then mushed me in the side of my head.

I busted out with laughter. I teased him, saying, "I told you, you're an alcoholic. See how mad you got over that drink?"

"Nah, man. Me and my girl just got into it last night over that same shit. Before I go to the bathroom, I tell her to order me another drink. I come back and this crazy bitch ordered me gin on the rocks. I almost threw up when I sipped that shit. I was like, how the fuck this bitch don't know what I drink as many times as we been out together? Damn, I don't drink but one kind of liquor." "That is pretty bad. Sorry, I didn't know. She should know you a little better. Next time you're with her, ask her what color your eyes are." I figured that would be the true test. There was no way anyone could miss those big brown eyes. Hell, that was one of his greatest assets.

"My eyes? What? I don't even know what color my eyes are."

Damn, that's crazy, I thought to myself. "They're brown, Touch. Haven't you noticed your eyes are a tad bit brighter than the average black person? I mean, they aren't hazel, but they are definitely not the average dark brown eyes. Here look." I searched my bag for my MAC compact then pulled it out to hand it to him.

He pushed my hand away. "Hell nah. Put that shit up."

"Come on, look." I opened the compact and shoved it in front of his face.

"Go 'head, man. Stop playing." Touch struggled to take the compact away from me.

"What's the matter? You too cool to look into a woman's compact at a bar?" I laughed. I finally gave up and put the compact back in my bag.

"You full of games, I see. Well, I got a game for ya, joke-sta," Touch said in an I-dare-you-to-play-along tone.

"Okay, what's up?" I quickly accepted the challenge.

"We gon' play a drinking game—"

"Oh, hell nah!" I yelled, cutting him off. That was definitely a challenge I would lose. I was always up for a fight, but I knew suicide when I was faced with it.

"Gotdamn! Hear me out, homie. The game is not about who can drink the most. I already know I got your little buck-and-a-quarter ass beat when it comes to that. The game is, you order my drinks, and I order yours, and no matter what the next person orders you have to drink it. Cool?"

"Okay, but no off-the-wall shit."

"A'ight, drink up. After we're done with these drinks, the game begins."

I swallowed my drink down, and Touch threw out the straw from his Grey Goose and took the drink to the head.

"Yo!" He flagged down the waitress then signaled for me to order when she arrived.

I looked at all the different liquors that sat behind the bar. "Let me get, uuummmm . . . a shot of piss," I said. Then Touch and I burst out laughing at the same time.

The waitress said nothing. She just stood there with a puzzled look on her face. She probably thought we were already drunk.

"I'm joking. I'm joking," I said, noticing the waitress was starting to get a little impatient with our foolishness. "Let me get a shot of tequila, the one with the worm. Matter of fact, if possible, can we get the worm in the glass?"

The waitress shook her head, as if to say okay, then looked at Touch for his order.

"Let me get a Long Island Ice Tea."

"Thanks," I said, feeling as though Touch had given me a pass on the first round. I was surprised that he'd ordered it. I was expecting something crazy like I'd ordered for him. I knew he only drank clear liquors, so I was expecting him to pitch a fit right away over the tequila, but he didn't even seem moved by my order.

The waitress came back and placed our drinks in front of us. We switched drinks, and Touch downed his first. Then I began to sip on mine.

"Whew!" I said after the first sip.

"Yeah, nigga." Touch sang. "Thought you was getting off easy, didn't you? It's about five different liquors in that shit. Drink up." He laughed.

We laughed and joked as Touch waited for me to finish my drink. I was down to my final sips, and I really felt like I could go no farther. I was really feeling the effects of the liquor.

As a stall tactic, I decided I'd take a little bathroom break. "I'll be back," I said. "I gotta tinkle." I pushed my stool away from the bar.

I looked myself over in the full-sized bathroom mirror. My eyes were glassy, a sure sign of intoxication. I made my way to the handicapped bathroom. Of course, I was nowhere near handicapped, but those bathrooms were always so spacious. So whenever I had the option, the handicapped bathroom was my first choice. I hung my purse on the hook that was posted to the back of the door. After struggling to get my pants down, I squatted over the toilet seat. That was the biggest challenge of all. I was so tipsy, I couldn't even squat steadily.

With the forceful flow of urine, I got pee all over the seat, and even some on the floor. I couldn't do anything but laugh as I pressed my hands firmly against the walls beside me to try to hold my balance. Once done, I flushed the toilet and cleaned up the area around me nicely.

As I stepped out of the restroom, an older white lady shot me an evil look as she leaned against the wall, her arms crossed. Ignoring her, I walked right past to the sink and began to wash my hands.

I could hear her mumble from the restroom stall, "You don't look handicapped to me."

Neither do you, I thought in my head, but chose to respond, "I'm not."

I began to fix my make up and straighten my hair when I heard the toilet flush. I rushed to finish touching myself up so that I wouldn't have to stand next to the rude lady as she washed her hands. Just as I finished applying my lip-gloss, the lady came limping from the bathroom, one leg shorter than the other.

She groaned then positioned herself against the sink so that she could wash her hands. "Well, if you're not handicapped then stay out the bathroom."

"Okay, so I used the handicapped bathroom. Sorry— Write me a fucking ticket!" I then pranced out the bathroom, taking extra-long steps like a runway model.

Normally, I would have felt bad and been very apologetic, but I'd had my share of rude white bitches for one day, and I think, more than anything, the alcohol was talking. Besides, how many times has anyone really been in the restroom using the handicapped stall and someone handicapped was actually waiting? I don't know about you, but it was a first for me.

Touch greeted me as soon as I walked out the bathroom. "Jewel, come over here. I want you to meet someone. This is my boy, Calico."

I almost swallowed my tongue as I looked at the person before me, realizing it was the guy I'd seen near the nail shop earlier in the day. "Hello. Nice to meet you. I'm Jewel."

I extended my hand, and this flawless man before me grabbed my hand and kissed it. "Hello, beautiful. Same to you."

I only prayed that I didn't look as drunk as I felt. I cut my eyes in Touch's direction to say, "Help."

In his best drunken mannerism, Touch tried his best to find out what was wrong. "Jewel, are you feeling okay? Do you need to sit down or something? You look crazy."

"Shut up," I said softly between clenched teeth as I got comfortable on the bar stool to his right.

Touch directed his attention to his friend that sat on his left. I couldn't believe my luck. I didn't know what to do. I wanted this man, but I was so drunk, I hadn't a leg to stand on.

I snatched out my cell and sent a mass text message to all my girls. I had a special distribution list for emergencies just like this one. I needed some advice, and fast. I sent them a quick message that read:

> OMG grls I need hlp! I'm drunk & there's a dude here I'm tryn 2 impress. Wht do I do? Dnt wnt 2 make fool of self.

It took less than a minute before the responses started rolling in. The first text received was from Sasha. It read:

> Do nothing. Leave. Guys come dime a dozen. U got enuff on the team. Besides, I need 2 c u neway.

I thought to myself, *Typical response. That's why you home with the broke-ass boyfriend right now.*

I went to delete Sasha's text just as fast as I had opened it, but before I could even hit the erase button, she sent another message:

Ur @ a bar every1 is drunk. Just go talk 2 him. He's prob drunk 2.

That was two strikes.

The final text was from my girl Shakira. I prayed this was the answer.

Is he there w/friends? If so u have 2 stall. Drink a RedBull and order food 2 try 2 sober up then talk to him. Or on ur way out have waitress send him a drink and your #.

Finally, some advice I could use. I began to text Shakira back when Touch grabbed my phone.

"What you so busy doing over here?"

"Nothing that concerns you. Now can you kindly give me my phone back, Touch?" I reached for my phone.

"Nah." He put my phone in his pocket then stood up.

"Damn, you that drunk just off two drinks?" I said, observing how childish he was acting.

"Hell nah," he said loud enough for his friend to hear as he headed to the men's restroom. "I had two more shots while you were in the bathroom."

I noticed his friend was laughing. "That's so not true."

While Touch was in the restroom, his friend came over to chat with me.

"Oh shit," I said to myself as he came over. I didn't get the chance to order a Red Bull. I saw an unopened can sitting in front Touch's stool, so I grabbed it, opened it, and took a big gulp.

"I didn't catch your name," he said as he sat next to me.

"I didn't throw it," I snapped back. *What a corny response,* I thought. *I need another gulp of Red Bull.* " I felt like an idiot as I took another gulp, nearly finishing the whole can.

"Well, you may want to throw it, because I don't wear the catcher's mitt for too long," his friend said, completely throwing me off.

Hold up? I know this nigga ain't coming out his mouth sideways. Does he think he's flier than me or something? "Excuse me," I said, trying to make sure the liquor didn't have me tripping.

"I'm saying. I'm not the type to chase a broad—"

"Broad? You obviously don't know who the fuck I am. Please, baby, check my resume. I don't wear the 'broad' title, boo. But since you think you're fly, let me kick something to you. Yeah, no doubt, I was interested; I was even gonna put you on the team. But you wasn't even gonna be the star player, baby. Sad to say, you were gonna ride the bench. But don't worry, I would have pulled you off when another nigga was injured—well, his pockets, that is." I looked at him like he was a lil' bitch then pulled out my American Express Black card.

I then called for the waitress. "You can wrap the tab up, baby," I told her. I handed her the card then gave Touch's friend a condescending smirk.

Just then Touch walked up. I don't know if it was the fumes rising from my head that sent that nigga a smoke signal or if he saw tears in his boy's eyes, but as soon as he walked up, he could tell something was definitely wrong.

Touch stood beside me. "What the fuck going on, bay?"

"Ask your disrespectful-ass friend." I looked his boy straight in the face.

"Gotdamn, Calico, what the fuck you say to her?"

"Man, it's this area. I can't kick it with these East Coast bitches. They just don't see it the California way."

"What the fuck he say 'bout me?" I asked, when I heard him say *California*.

"Is your name *California*?"

"Yes, the fuck it is."

Touch noticed the stupid-ass look on his boy's face. "Yeah, it is, for real, man. California is her first name. She just go by Jewel. Look, I'm 'bout to order another round. Everybody cool out and have a drink," Touch suggested, assuming liquor was the answer to everything.

"Let me get this one. What you having, Miss California Jewel?" Calico said, offering me a truce drink.

"I don't accept drinks from people I don't know," I said with a slight smile.

He began to say, "I'm sorry—"

"Oh, I know you sorry . . . sorry-ass nigga." I just had to take that. I owed him one. "I'm joking, sweetie," I said, seeing the winkles of disapproval in his forehead. "Okay, let's start from the beginning."

"I'm Calico," he said as he extended his hand.

Now just being a spoiled-ass little bitch for the hell of it, I folded my arms and refused to shake his hand. I wanted to be sure I had the upper hand.

"Come on, don't do this to me," he begged.

I still refused, pushing it a little further.

"Yo, you just make a nigga wanna . . ." He paused and took a deep breath, as though he was trying to refrain from doing something terrible. Then he added, "You just make a nigga wanna hug your little ass," then grabbed me tight.

Totally surprised by his actions, we all laughed together.

Damn, I'm glad this nigga hugged me and didn't haul off and hit me, I thought, realizing I would have been caught totally off guard and probably knocked the fuck out.

Now that things were back on track, I figured I'd better wrap things up. I needed to get his number and get the hell out of dodge. I started a little small talk as I waited for the perfect time to execute.

Meanwhile, Calico ordered a round of Cuervo 1800. The last thing I needed was another drink, but I didn't want to take the risk of insulting him by turning it down. So, on the count of three, we all tapped glasses and threw the drinks down.

"Okay, that's it for me, fellas," I said as I attempted to stand up.

"Oh no, you don't." Calico grabbed my purse. "Friends don't let friends drive drunk," he said between laughs.

"Whatever! I'm not your friend, so it's okay to let me drive," I said sarcastically.

"Damn, are you always this vicious or just when you're drunk?" Calico asked.

"I'm a Scorpio, baby. We never stop."

"Well, Scorpio, I'm not letting you drive. I'll take you home."

I looked at Calico from head to toe. I thought back to the first time I'd seen him. *Boy, you just don't know. If you came home with me tonight, you'll be handing over the keys to your Benz tomorrow. As horny and drunk as I am, who knows the tricks I would turn tonight?* My thoughts were interrupted by Touch's call.

"Jewel, come on, I'm taking you home." He pulled my hand with his right hand, and my purse sat comfortable on his left wrist, just like it belonged there.

Calico followed behind us as we walked to my truck. Touch unlocked the door and threw my purse and cell phone on the driver's seat.

I climbed in the passenger side and began to fumble with my iPod as I waited for him to gather some things from his car.

"Oh shit," I yelled as Calico tapped on my window, nearly scaring me to death.

He opened the door. "Let me see your phone."

I reached over and grabbed my phone from the driver's seat and handed it to him without hesitation. I'd been a bitch enough for the night. Now it was time to settle down and handle business.

Calico entered and stored his number, called his phone, then handed me my phone back. "Can I get a call tomorrow?" he asked.

The words, "You sure can," slurred from my tongue, as my head began to spin.

"Cool. Have a good night, sweetie." Calico buckled me in and closed the door.

Touch hopped in and gave Calico a wave as we pulled out of the parking lot.

As quickly as we pulled out, I was knocked out. When I opened my eyes we were in front of my home.

"Come on, drunken monkey." Touch dragged me from the truck and into the house.

As soon as I opened the door, I was met by a ringing house phone. My head still spinning, I couldn't make it past where Touch had laid me on the couch.

Touch grabbed a pillow and blanket for me and placed the pillows beneath my head, and the blanket over my body. "You need anything?" He grabbed a Heineken from the refrigerator and popped it open.

I noticed my cell phone was now ringing off the hook. "My purse."

Touch passed me my purse then headed to my bathroom to relieve himself yet again.

By the time I'd pulled my phone from my purse, I'd missed the call. I looked at my list of missed calls. I had ten missed calls, seven from Sasha, and three from a private number that I was sure was Sasha as well. *Damn! I forgot to give her that money I promised.* I immediately called her back.

"What the hell are you doing?" Sasha said as soon as she picked up.

"Cut this bullshit right now. I'm drunk," I snapped back.

"Obviously," Sasha stated. "When are you going home?"

"I am home."

"I'm on my way," she said, as though I'd invited her to come over or something. Then she hung up.

Touch sat an empty garbage can next to me and finished up his Heineken. "You straight?"

"Yeah, I'm good. Sasha is on her way."

"Good. 'Cause ol' girl is blowing my phone up. I'm out, bay." Touch gave me a hug then set the alarm to the house and locked the door behind him.

"You stink!"

I thought I was dreaming, until I opened my eyes to a tiny blurred butter pecan five-foot frame with curly hair that stood before me. As my vision cleared, I saw Sasha standing in front of me, her hands on her hips. Not wanting to be bothered with her nonsense, I immediately grabbed my purse and pulled out my wallet. I didn't say a word to her as I counted the cash in my purse. Seeing that I only had three hundred in cash, I pulled out my checkbook.

"Uh-uh." Sasha shook her head. "Don't write me no check."

"All I got is three hundred on me, Sasha. I figured if you came all the way out here in the middle of the night, you would expect to leave with the entire amount." Personally, I figured it wasn't that serious and she could have waited until the next day.

I guess she thought the same thing when she replied, "I'll just get it tomorrow," and then walked into the bathroom.

I could hear the water running from the bathtub faucet shortly after. Sasha yelled from the bathroom, "Who the hell been here?"

"How the hell you get in here?" I answered with a question, realizing I didn't let her in.

"I used the spare hidden beneath the rock. Now back to my question, please."

"And the alarm?"

"One, two, three, four. You use the same pass code for everything, bank account pin number, voice mail, alarm.

I mumbled loud enough for Sasha to hear, "Umph. Note to self, change all pass codes tomorrow, especially voice mail."

"Jewel, I know a nigga been here. So who was it?" she asked again.

"Why?"

"I know you ain't bring that nigga home from the bar." Sasha walked back into the living room.

"You think you know so fucking much, don't you?" I sat up on the couch and headed into the bathroom.

Sasha was right on my heels. "So who was it, Jewel?"

"Gotdamit! It was Touch." I realized Sasha wasn't gonna let it rest. "Is this for me?" I touched the water that filled the bathtub to test the warmth then turned the faucet off.

"Yes."

I got undressed and slowly stepped in the steaming hot water. Once I got comfortable in the tub, I rested my head against the bath pillow and closed my eyes.

A few minutes later Sasha returned. She reached over me and grabbed the shea butter body wash and loofah sponge. She lathered the sponge and began to wash my body.

Five minutes later I was rinsing the soap off and wrapping my bath up. I dried off, threw on a robe, and gave my teeth a much-needed brushing, and rinsing with Listerine. Now it was definitely time for bed.

I walked into the bedroom and took off my robe, sliding in bed beside a naked Sasha, who wrapped her arm around me and began licking the lobe of my left ear.

I grabbed her arm and gently placed it beside her and rolled over. I did it for a few of reasons. One, I was drunk as hell and not in the mood. We had gotten down like this once before, and it was good, but I really didn't prefer the girl-on-girl thing. And, two, I was no trick. I didn't need a fuck to give her that money she asked for.

"What's wrong with you?"

"Nothing. Go to sleep, Sasha."

"Go to sleep? Do I look like a child to you?"

"No, but sometimes you act like one."

Sasha had turned me off from the time she'd walked in the door, not to mention how she irritated me with this whole quit-my-career job-to-take-up-dancing decision she'd made earlier in the day.

I'd first met Sasha about a year and a half ago. I had gone with one of the niggas from my team to the club she happened to work at. It was time for her act as we walked in. She was sexy and turned me on. Our eyes were locked on each other her entire performance.

When she was done with her set, she came over, and we talked for a while. She even gave my dude a lap-dance. When I was getting ready to leave, she wrote her cell phone number on a napkin and gave it to me, telling me that I could call her anytime.

I always tried to take a picture of a new person I was putting in my phone, so I know who's calling. When I asked her to pose for the picture, she turned around and bent down, showing me her thong and fat ass. I laughed at the gesture, took the picture and then gave her my number. The next day, she called me and invited me to come to the mall with her. The rest is history.

When I'd first met her, everything was cool for a while, but it seemed like the more I learned about her and the closer we got, the more she turned me off. And this particular night, her mouth was really pushing me over the edge.

Sasha sat up in the bed and began to yell, "What? Who the fuck do you think you're talking to?"

"You notice you're the only one yelling? You might want to bring it down a couple of notches and stop cussing at me." I constantly had to remind Sasha to watch the way she talked to me. Besides being with a tired-ass man, her anger was her biggest downfall.

Sasha let out a big sigh and flopped back down on the bed. I could hear her sniffles, a true sign she was crying. *Fuck! Now I got to kiss this bitch ass!* "Why you crying, Boobie?" I rolled over and pulled her close to me.

"I'm just so stressed-out. I know you don't deserve to be talked to like that. You never cuss or yell at me. You're always so calm no matter how much I go off. I'm sorry, Jewel."

"It's all good," I said, although deep down inside I really wanted to tell her about herself.

"That's why I love you."

Sasha rolled on top of me and kissed me passionately, her kisses traveling from my lips to my breast and ending with an explosion between my thighs. "Sweet dreams," she whispered in my ears and wiped my wetness from her lips.

Chapter 2

"Truth Be Told"

Sasha

"Jewel, your phone," I mumbled, bothered by the constant ring of her house phone. She didn't even budge as I sat up in the bed and looked around the room for the cordless phone.

My first thought was the nightstand. "Nope, not there," I said to myself as I continued to search. The phone wasn't on the cradle, but I could hear it was near. I noticed the time as I glanced at the clock on the nightstand. It was nine o'clock in the morning. *Who the hell would be calling Jewel so persistently and so early on a damn Saturday?*

Shit never seemed right from the night before, so I made it my business to find out who was calling. I got out of the bed and followed the sound of the ringing phone. It led me to the walk-in closet. I opened the closet door and saw the phone sitting on top of some shoeboxes.

I shook my head as I picked the phone up. For a chick that always complained she didn't have shit to wear, she surely had an overflowing closet. I shuffled through a few pair of jeans that still had the tags on them, two hundred thirty dollars was the cheapest pair. Hell, that was about how much I owed on my past due phone bill.

As I walked out the closet, I scanned through the caller ID to see who had been calling all morning. I flipped to the last person that called and stopped there. The caller ID read: Griffith, Shakira.

"Shakira Griffith," I said, knowing exactly who it was. "Jewel." I walked over to the bed and shook her as though I was trying to give her shaken baby syndrome.

Jewel sat up and looked at me as though she wanted to smack me. "What, Sasha, what?"

"The feeling's mutual, mama," I said, letting her know I was just as pissed as she was. "Why the fuck is skank-ass Paradise calling you?" I addressed Shakira by her dance name purposely, trying to demean her.

"Why not? And why the fuck you all in my caller ID?" Jewel stood up and snatched the phone from my hand.

Her sexy, naked frame caught my eye for a second, but it wasn't enough to distract my focus from the conversation at hand. She knew damn well how I felt about Paradise, and I wasn't gonna let this shit ride.

Paradise to the strip scene, Shakira Griffith was a young chick that Jewel and I both knew from the strip club. She and Jewel claimed they had this "little sister-big sister" friendship, but I'd always believed it was more to it.

I for one knew exactly how those so-called "sister" friendships worked. I was once like Paradise, young, fresh, and naïve to the strip world. Then my girl Ceazia came and took me under her wing. She was a big sister to me too. Until we became lovers. She was my first and would have been my only, if she hadn't had passed away.

So when I saw the way Jewel and Paradise made eye contact with each other when Paradise was on stage dancing, I knew exactly what was about to come of their so-called sisterly friendship. It was as though they were the only two people in the club and no one else mattered. They acted like they wanted to jump on top of each other right then and there, a look that was way too familiar to me. Because it was the same attraction that me and Jewel shared when we'd first met. And to think they had the nerve to say Paradise didn't even swing that way. Well, one thing for sure, if she wasn't already there, she was on her way.

"Why the fuck is she calling, Jewel?" I asked again following Jewel into the bathroom.

"That's what friends do, Sasha. Don't you call?"

"Are you insinuating that we are on the same level? If so, I can take that one or two ways—Either I'm just a friend, or she's your lover. So which one is it, Jewel?"

I grabbed a robe for myself and handed another one to her, and we both threw them on.

"No. You are crazy." She laughed and shook her head as she began to brush her teeth.

I didn't know if Jewel was intentionally trying to rub me the wrong way or what, but she was really starting to piss me off. "You're right, I am crazy. I'm crazy for thinking I could trust your ass. I should have known what was up from the jump. I mean, I did meet you at the strip club."

After Jewel rinsed her mouth and washed her face, she said, "So what?"

"So, I had to be crazy for hollering at someone from the strip club. Just like you had me, now you're scoping out the next bitch, Paradise."

"I had you? More like you had me. Did you forget you were my first? You sought me, Sasha."

"Yeah, and now it's like you've lost your fucking mind.

You got a taste, and now you're so confident, you're seeking pussy, huh? Yeah, I had to be crazy to think you and I could really have something."

"What? Are you serious? Nah, boo. You crazy for being with that nothing-ass nigga of yours." Jewel headed into the living room.

I couldn't believe Jewel went there. I knew she always wanted to say something about Rick. I was just waiting for the day. "You happy? You finally said it. You finally got it off those thirty-six D's. Do you feel better now? I knew you felt that way about him anyway."

"Oh, that's just the beginning. To be honest, I think he is less than a man. You haven't been the same since he moved in with you—You don't keep yourself up, you always broke, you never go out. On the real, I hardly even talk to you. It's like you gotta sneak and call or something, and when you do call, it's because you need something." Jewel paused then shook her head. "And how the fuck you got a nigga living with you, yet you got to dance in Atlanta just to keep from losing your house? What good is a nigga if he can't do shit for you? What you want—dick? Dick don't pay the bills, boo."

I finally had to tell Jewel how I felt about her using men for money. "I'm sorry, I don't fuck for money—I fuck for love. That 'gaming-a-nigga' shit is your style."

"Ha-ha-ha!" Jewel laughed as though I'd told a hilarious joke. "Baby, let me explain something to you. Listen carefully because this is some real knowledge I'm about spit to you. But, before I begin let me just say, don't forget where you came from. If I'm not mistaken, gaming a nigga is how you got your money back in the day. Now, before I get down to business, let me just point out a few things to you. I drive a Range Rover, I own my own condo in a gated community here in Kempsville Greens, and I am a ghostwriter but have a background in certified medical billing and coding. I have a closet full of designer labels, and I have investments and a nice chunk of savings. I have no children and have no problem paying my bills. And all this comfort at a sweet age of twenty-three. So I think we all can agree that I am accomplished.

"Now, my secret to success is, I started with me. I made sure I had something solid that I could always fall back on. I have an education and a career. Then I used the power of my beauty and my booty to take things to the next level. If you want to call it fucking for money, fine, but I beg to differ. One of the standards I have for my men is that they have money, and plenty of it. So the way I see it, mami, if you wanna fuck for love, love his money. Or, better yet, fuck for the love of money. Phrase it however you like, but you better get with it."

Jewel ran down the law to me like she had invented the game herself.

"Well, Rick was there for me for five years when he had money, and now just because he's down, you want me to kick him out? And, did we forget, this is my baby father we're talking about?"

"Nope, not at all. But you need to do you. Fuck that nigga. He can't even take care of his son." Jewel walked over to answer her ringing cell phone.

I walked up to her and began staring her in the face. "We're in the middle of a conversation, Jewel. That shit can wait."

She attempted to answer. "Hello?"

"Give me the muthafuckin' phone." I tried grabbing the phone from her ear.

"Hello?" she called out again. She directed her attention back to me after realizing she'd missed the call. "Yo, you are really bugging."

"I know you fucking that bitch Paradise too," I said. Since I'd been speaking my mind all morning, there was no sense in holding that in.

"Your mind is real fucked-up, Sasha!"

"Fuck you!" I yelled. That's all I could form my mouth to say.

"Besides, if I'm fucking Shakira, why are you here?" Jewel gave me a plain look.

"You right," I said without thinking, and began to get dress.

It took all I had to keep my tears in. There was no way I was going to let Jewel see me cry. I had my clothes on in two minutes flat and was headed out the door.

She yelled, "Key, please," as soon as I opened the door.

I reached in my pocket and pulled out the single key and tossed it on the counter. I ran to my car and rushed out the neighborhood.

I pulled in the gas station on the corner and burst into tears. I didn't know what was wrong. So much was running through my mind at once. I loved Jewel, but I just didn't feel like she loved me the same. Little did she know, if she just loved me whole-heartedly, I would leave Rick and be with her. But she would rather fuck a nigga for money than kick it with me.

I couldn't help but compare our relationship with my relationship with Ceazia, a lover and my best friend that I loved her with all my heart. I would've done anything for her. My relationship with Jewel was almost similar to my last one, but for the life of me, I just couldn't understand why she didn't feel the same. Then to think she may be the first to sleep with Paradise was even more nerve-wracking.

I knew Jewel had my back in time of need, but I just didn't feel that connection I wanted. Here I was crying over her, but I was sure she had never shed a tear over me. Hell, at times I even felt like she resented me, or like I just wasn't good enough. It was like I lived in her shadow or something.

From the time I'd met her, everything was so perfect for her. And it seemed like every chance she got, she was throwing it in my face. *"Fuck that nigga. Dick don't pay the bills. I drive a Range Rover."* Blah, blah, blah. My pity began to turn to anger, the more I thought.

"Fuck that shit. Jewel is no better than me," I said, giving myself a pep talk. "Little does she know, easy come, easy go. Just as fast as she got on top, in a blink of an eye, she could be on the bottom. And when she hit, I'll be sure to be on top, so then it will be me she'll be crying to."

That was all the motivation I needed. My mind was made up. I was going to get on the grind, dancing in Atlanta and New York, and get shit back to the way it used to be.

I wiped my face and got myself together then looked above, asking Ceazia, who was now my angel above, for help. "I need you, *C*. I know you got my back."

Chapter 3

"Bag That Bitch"

Calico

I answered the phone on the final ring, in an attempt not to seem too anxious. "Hello?"

"What's up?" Jewel sang from the other end.

"Nothing much. What's up witchu?" I remembered how drunk she was the previous night. "You feeling all right?"

"Yeah, I'm good. I may have had a slight hangover when I woke up, but I had so much drama this morning, I wouldn't have even noticed," she said, sounding a bit agitated.

I sensed her stress. "Damn! Sounds like you need to do something nice for the rest of the day to make you forget about your morning."

Jewel jumped at the opportunity. "Any suggestions?"

"Well, I was going to the outlet to grab a few things. You want to roll?"

"Potomac Mills?" she asked.

Her response let me know off the top what type of spending she was interested in. "Nah, Williamsburg."

"Calico, there aren't any really good stores there. Have you even tried Potomac Mills?"

"Nah," I said, playing stupid. "Where is it?"

"Up I-95 North, like you going towards DC."

"That's too far, baby. I'm just trying to shoot there and shoot back."

Jewel realized she was fighting a losing battle and finally gave in. She gave me her address, and I agreed to pick her up at two o'clock, which gave me time to take care of a few things before we left.

"Hello?" Jewel answered in a sultry tone.

"I'm out front," I replied, Shawty Lo's "Dey Know" blasting in the background.

"I'm coming out now."

I watched as Jewel walked toward the car. Her lips seemed extra lip-gloss shiny. She was sexy as hell, dressed in a white stretched tank top that accented her perky breasts, and matching white jeans that were so tight, if she bent over, I could see the print of her pussy lips.

"Hey, miss lady." I greeted her with a hug. *Damn, your ass is phat!* I thought as she sat her perfectly round ass down on the black leather passenger seat of my black drop-top. My dick was getting hard by the minute.

I looked at Jewel's full lips again and started to imagine myself getting my dick sucked, riding down the interstate with the music blasting. I looked her up from head to toe one last time, while pretending to look for a CD.

My peep show was interrupted by her yell and look of disgust. "CD's? Are you serious?"

Confused, I asked, "What? You want to listen to the radio or something?"

"No, boo. iPod," she replied with that same sassiness she was giving me last night.

"Oh, I forgot who I was dealing with. Sorry, miss prima donna. I don't have an iPod," I said as I inserted Jay-Z.

"Well, the next time we meet, please have one. So are we still going to the Williamsburg Outlets?" She asked as though I'd changed my mind or something.

"Yeah, I wish we could go further, but I have some business to take care of later on tonight," I said, a mischievous grin on my face as I checked out her smile.

"All right, what's so funny?"

"Nothing. I'm feeling the wife-beater on you. That's real gangster for a diva like you. All you need is a fresh pair of Air Force One's to match." I took another look at her.

"For the record, fresh white Prada's, not Nike's. And thank you for the compliment, but honestly, I think I look a little fat." Jewel grinned back at me.

"What? You're crazy." I took this as an opportunity to look her over quickly. "You have a killer frame."

"No, honey. I have one of those borderline frames. I'm one Slim-Fast away from Beyoncé, and one burger away from *America's Next Top Model* contestant, Toccara."

We both laughed.

"Look, let me tell you something about skinny chicks. Don't no man want a skinny chick. For one, no one knows how she got that way. The bitch could be sick. The way I see it, give me a fat bitch. At least I know she healthy," I said.

We both laughed uncontrollably.

"You enjoy yourself at the bar last night?" I asked, changing the subject as we headed toward 64 West.

"Yes, I did, but I don't do the whole bar scene too often."

"I know." I nodded at her.

"How so?"

"Well, it was one of the first things I noticed. I meet Touch at that spot all the time, and last night was the first time I'd seen you. If you hung out at the bars often, I'm sure I would have seen you there before."

"Yeah, clubs, bars, and lounges aren't really my thing. All it consists of is guys wishing they could get a second to talk to you, and the girls, you know how that goes, they wish they could get a second to talk to a nice guy. But when he doesn't want to holler at her, she will hate all night on the chick that can accomplish what she can't."

"Well, I will let you know right now that I've never been turned down," I said with plenty of confidence.

"Neither have I."

We both gave each other a smirk.

Just then, Sean Kingston's "Beautiful Girls" started playing on the radio, and Jewel started singing to the lyrics.

"You're way too beautiful
That's why it'll never work
You had me suicidal, suicidal
When you say it's over"

She sang like the song was talking about her specifically.

I gave Jewel a playful shove in the head. "You ain't gon' have nobody suicidal."

"Whatever. We'll see about that." She rolled her eyes and neck in unison then said to me, "Tell me about yourself."

"It's not much to tell. My name is Calico, and I'm from Los Angeles, California. My pops was a drug dealer-turned-entrepreneur. He had a hot lil' jewelry spot in LA back in the day, but when we had those riots back in ninety-two, he lost everything. For the first time, my father couldn't provide for his family. He tried everything to get back on his feet. Everything, except going to back to the dope game. He'd promised my mother that once he was out, he would never go back to it. Eventually my father could no longer take the pressure of not being able to provide for his family, so he drank himself to death, and my mother slowly but surely picked up the pieces.

"Seeing my mom struggle as a kid really fucked me up, so I decided I was going to be the man of the house. I automatically had respect on the streets because of my father's street cred. After some good deals came through that put real money in my pocket, I stepped up to the plate and took care of the house. Still, my mother has never been the same. I can't tell you the last time I've seen her truly happy."

"Any brothers or sisters?"

"Yeah, I have an older brother and sister. I'm the baby. I will let you know now, I'm a serious momma's boy. Whatever momma wants, that woman gets."

"Of course, I understand. So you and Touch are good friends?"

I felt like I was under interrogation as Jewel came at me with question after question. "We're more like business partners, splitting the profits right down the middle." I then turned the tables on her. "What do you do?"

"Right now, I'm a ghostwriter full-time. Yesterday, I was a medical biller and coder. Tomorrow, I'll be the girl of your dreams, and soon after that, I'll be running that part of the business you have with Touch," Jewel said without a doubt.

I grinned. "Damn! You got big dreams, shorty." I knew there was no way in hell she could ever reach any of those dreams she had set for tomorrow and thereafter.

Jewel looked me directly in my eyes and gave me a seductive look. "It's not a dream, baby." She paused and gently caressed my chin. "It's very, very real." She ended the statement with a kiss into the air.

I took a swallow in an attempt to break the trance she had just put me in. She watched and gave a slight smile, as though she knew what I was thinking.

"So,"—My voice cracked, making me clear my throat— "do you make a lot of money ghostwriting?"

"Yes, you can. It depends on who you write for, and how many jobs you get. The job can be tiring at times, but I enjoy it."

"Is it hard?" I asked, really intrigued by her profession.

"Not really, but I feel as if my job is never complete. I'm only as good as the last song that I wrote."

"So why not just be a rapper? I thought everybody wanted to be a rapper."

"Yeah, when they're like thirteen. Rapping is not for me. I could never get on stage and perform like that. I'm more of a behind-the-scenes type of chick. I'm good without the fame. I already got my share of it. All I want is my check, you feel me?" Jewel chuckled.

"I heard that. You already got your fame, huh? A'ight, miss local celebrity." I laughed.

Jewel snapped back, "No, baby. I'm a star wherever I go."

"Damn, girl. One thing about you that I'm gonna have to get used to is that mouth." I shook my head, wondering if it was really possible for me to get used to it.

"That's me. You have to accept everything about me, smart mouth and all. Take it or leave it. I put it all out there straight, no chaser. Now it's up to you to decide what you want."

"I'll take it." I laughed, knowing I could break her little ass down to Reese's Pieces in a matter of days.

Jewel joined in on my laughter. "I know."

Time passed by quickly as we talked and laughed together, and before I knew it, we were at the Williamsburg Outlet. I parked and opened the door for Jewel.

"What store do you want to start at first?" she asked.

"Lead the way. I'm with you," I replied with a smile that consisted of a upper blue and white diamond grill.

I followed Jewel as she headed to our first stop, the BCBG store. Next, we hit Michael Kors. Then we hit a few stores for me, like the Timberland store, Cole Haan, Izod, Nike Factory, and Vans. After that, we were back to California's picks, Guess, Coach, Perfume World, and Sunglass World. Knowing that Jewel was watching my every move, I didn't complain the entire time. I never even lifted an eyebrow, no matter how much her total ran up to.

"Before we leave, I want to hit Gymboree and Nautica," Jewel requested.

"Gymboree? Isn't that a kids' store?"

"Yes, it is."

"I didn't know you had kids," I stated.

"I don't."

With a puzzled look on my face, I began to wonder if Jewel was straight trying to play me for a sucker. I watched as she picked up little girls' clothing, two of each. My first reaction was to cuss her ass out, but I chose to roll with it. I figured at least I could get a fuck out of it, if nothing else. I prepared to pay as we reached the counter.

"Thank you for your generosity, but I got this one."

Jewel's response surprised me. "So who's it for?" I asked out of curiosity.

"Touch's twin girls."

"Oh yeah? Y'all tight like that?"

"Yep! Tighter than these jeans I have on." Jewel laughed.

As I watched her ass bounce with each step, I thought, *Damn! And my nigga ain't never tried to fuck that?*

"I want cookies and cream on a waffle cone," she said like a kid at the ice cream truck as we passed Ben & Jerry's.

"Come on, baby, I know you don't want that junk. I'm in the mood for steak." I looked at my watch.

"Okay," she quickly agreed. "Steak is better than ice cream on any day."

"Unless that day happens to be the day you get your tonsils taken out." We both laughed.

"So, are we eating here or back near the beach?" Jewel asked as we loaded the bags into the trunk of the car.

"It's up to you."

"Ummm, the beach. I don't know much about this area, except the Outlet stores."

"Okay." I took her right hand and kissed it. "Well, let's go get lady Jewel her filet mignon."

Chapter 4

"Baby Momma Drama"

Touch

I spotted my homeboy Calico as soon as I walked through the door of Mo Dean's Jamaican Restaurant and Lounge. "What up, ace."

"What up, fool." He gave me a hardy pound and pat on the back. "Yo, I'm-a tell you right now, your fucking baby momma in here, nigga, so put the brakes on."

"I ain't worryin' about her, man," I said, quickly glancing around the bar. It didn't take long for me to spot her. She sat at a booth on the other side of the place with her partner in crime, Monica, and a couple of their ghetto-fabulous girlfriends. I contemplated on whether or not I should just blow the joint. Knowing her ghetto ass, at first sight of me, she would want to make a scene, and I wasn't the one for drama. Still, I wasn't going to be intimidated by her, nor was I going to let her keep me from getting my drink on.

I grabbed a stool and sat in the corner, out of their sight.

The cute waitress with a phat ass wasted no time coming my way. "What can I get for you, Touch?"

I imagined bending her over and pounding that ass from the back. "A back shot," I said.

"Whatever, nigga! I'll be right back with your Grey Goose on the rocks," she said then walked off, her booty bouncing each step of the way.

For some reason I felt like she put an extra bounce in there just for me. She knew I would be looking as soon as she walked off. I pulled out a cigarette and lit it. I took a few pulls. *Damn*, I thought to myself, *I even have to take a smoke to mentally fuck this bitch. That shit is crazy.*

When the waitress came back with my drink, I told her, "Thank you, baby. I got you," letting her know I'd take care of my tab at the end of the night.

"Don't be trying to run out on me," she said playfully. "You know I'm supposed to hold your credit card."

"Come on, sweetheart."

It was a damn shame that I'd been going to that lounge nearly six months and this same waitress had always been there, but I didn't know her name. Me and the niggas always referred to her as the cute waitress with the phat ass.

"How you gon' play me like that? What's your name, ma?"

"Diana," she said, looking straight in my eyes.

"Okay, Diana, you win. I'll pay for my drinks as we go." I pulled out a twenty to pay for my drink.

"That's okay," she said, finally seeing shit my way. She pushed my hand away. "I'll see you at the end of the night."

Like with every first drink, I threw that shit down my throat in just a couple of swallows, and as soon as my empty glass hit the table, Diana was there.

"Ready for another one?"

"Yeah. Make this one a double shot," I requested.

"A'ight. I'll be right back."

Calico came over and grabbed a seat next to me. "You good, nigga?"

"Yeah, I'm straight."

"Gotdamn, nigga, you gon' make your baby momma force you to stay in the gotdamn corner all night?"

"Hell nah. She ain't forcing me to stay nowhere. I'm chilling, nigga. After a few drinks I'm out anyway."

"So how shit looking?" Calico wanted to know how quickly the coke he'd given me the day before was moving.

I told him, "Shit right, nigga. Cats loving this white girl. She different from the last one you gave me."

"A'ight. So when we talking?" Calico asked, referring to the one hundred fifty grand I owed him.

"In a few days I should be straight."

"Here you go," Diana said, interrupting our conversation. She winked an eye at Calico.

I noticed the double shot of Grey Goose on the rocks plus two shot glasses filled with liquor. "What's this?" I asked.

"Patrón. Let's take a shot together. It's on me."

I tried declining the drink the best way I knew how. "I don't do Patrón, ma."

Calico shook his head from side to side. "Man, go ahead and take the shot, nigga."

I thought back to the last time I had Patrón. I woke up on the steps of my mom's front porch, and my car was parked in the middle of her front yard. Patrón was definitely not my thing, and Calico knew it. I had to wonder if he was trying to set me up.

Diana folded her arms and gave me a slight pout. "Oh, so you gonna disappoint me like that?"

Calico said to Diana, "Give that man some motivation. A nigga ain't trying to take risks for nothing." Then he cut his eyes at me to take it from there. He'd set up the bait; now I just needed to catch the fish and reel her in.

I really never needed help bagging a girl, but Calico thought he would lend a hand. I figured since he had gone through all this trouble, I would at least play along and take the drink, so I played into the setup.

"I'm saying, if I get sick from this shit, who gon' take care of a nigga?"

Diana smiled. "I'll take full responsibility."

"Let's do it," I said, feeling Diana was down for whatever. We tapped glasses and downed the drinks.

"Damn!" The liquor felt like it was burning a path down my throat to my chest. I grabbed my Grey Goose and drank it as a chaser.

As I sipped my vodka, I looked over at Diana, who was whispering in Calico's ear. He didn't seem to be fazed by the tequila shot at all.

Diana diverted her attention back to me, while twirling the end of the braid of my cornrow between her fingers. "You okay, sweetie?"

"I could be better," I responded to her subtle flirtation.

"Well, can I help?" Diana licked her lips.

I grinned then glanced at Calico to see if he was picking up on the same vibes I was getting from her. He cut a small grin back as an indication that he was. Now that I knew this shit was real and it wasn't just the liquor talking, I fed right into the game she was playing.

"Yeah, but I'm-a need you to come with me to do that." I came on strong, to see if this bitch was really with it and not just talking shit, but she said exactly what I wanted to hear.

"A'ight. I get off in a couple of hours. Hang out and we can leave together."

As Diana walked away, Calico said, "Damn, Touch! It's like that, nigga?"

"It is what it is, baby."

We both laughed as I pulled out another cigarette.

I stood up to head to the bathroom and stumbled a bit on my first step. *That Patrón must really be getting to me*, I thought as I passed the booth that my baby mother and her girls sat at. I didn't even look in her direction as I went through the double doors leading to the bathrooms.

Before I could hang a left and go into the men's bathroom, I was stopped by a familiar five-foot five frame. I didn't say a word as I looked at her voluptuous breasts. My mind was too busy thinking about how nicely my dick would fit between them. Then I looked down to see a small hand massaging it softly. I opened my mouth to tell Diana to chill, but before I could get one word out, my mouth was filled with her tongue. I didn't even resist.

I ain't even the kissing type, especially not with a jump-off, but for some reason I was really feeling that shit this night. I moved my hands all over Diana's plump ass and between her ass cheeks. I couldn't wait to get inside her.

My first thought was to pull her into the men's bathroom and bend her over the sink and bang her out in there, but the real nigga in me just wouldn't let that shit happen. "Save this for later, ma," I said, and I pulled away from her and headed into the bathroom.

After relieving myself of the liquor I'd consumed, and the blood rush that Diana provoked, I washed my hands and headed out the door. Just like I was stopped going in, I was stopped coming out, but it wasn't as pleasant as the first time.

Ciara, my baby mother, said, "I know you saw me when you came back here."

Not even you can ruin this night, I thought, playing it cool with her to prevent argument. "Yeah, but I had to piss."

"Give me some money, Trayvon," Ciara said, addressing me by my government name. She felt my pockets to see if I had the usual wad of money in there.

Without protesting I pulled off five twenties, handed them to her, and walked away.

When I arrived back at my table, Calico was sitting there with a couple of chicks. I already had my meal planned for the night, so I chose to sit at the bar rather than disrupt him. Who knows, maybe he was trying to set up a little late-night snack for himself.

I sat at the bar playing the computer game as Diana constantly fed me drinks. Every time she passed by, she would either blow me a kiss, stick her tongue out seductively, or give me some other type of sexual notion. This bitch really had me going.

I pulled out one of my phones to check the time. *One o'clock. One hour to go,* I thought. I sat my phone on the bar beside me and turned my concentration back on my game.

My bothersome baby mother came over again just to annoy me. "Why you sitting over here instead of with your friends? What you looking for—some pussy?"

"Nah. I'm letting Calico get some time in with the hoes."

"Whatever," she said then walked off.

There was no way in hell I could tell Ciara what I was doing. That bitch would fuck up anything I had with another female. I never understood why Ciara acted such a damn fool. I hadn't slept with her, finger-fucked her, or even kissed her since I came home from jail nearly three years ago. Again I turned my attention back to my game.

Not even five minutes passed before my cell phone began to ring. I answered my girlfriend's call, "What's up?"

"What the fuck you mean, 'what's up'? Have you lost your mind, Touch? If you going to be with your baby mother every night, why don't you go live with her?" My girl went on and on.

"What the fuck you talking 'bout?" I asked as calmly as possibly. I looked around the bar to see if maybe my girl was at the lounge and assumed me and my baby mother were there together.

"I just got off the phone with Ciara, Touch. She called me from your other phone."

I looked around the bar for Ciara as I listened to my girl talk.

"She told me she was calling from your phone tonight to prove that are y'all are together."

I got a glimpse of Ciara sitting in the booth, looking in my direction, with a stupid-ass I'm-guilty smirk on her face. I hung up on my girl as I headed toward the booth.

Once I arrived at the table, Ciara was sitting there with my phone in her hand. She stared me dead in my eyes with a look that said, "Yeah, I did it. So what you gonna do about it?"

I wasn't that nigga that hit chicks, but if pushed, I would set a bitch straight quick. And this night I was just about seconds away from beating the shit out of Ciara. I ain't even bother to entertain her bullshit. I just snatched my phone out of her hand then walked out the club.

Diana and Calico both called out to me as I stormed out the front door. I didn't even pause to see what they wanted. I was fuming inside. I knew if I spent another five seconds in Ciara's presence I would end up at 811, better known as Norfolk City Jail.

I rushed to my crib to try and explain shit to my girl. As soon as I pulled up, I noticed little pieces of burning paper falling out the window. I figured she must be doing that shit chicks do when they get mad, like ripping and burning pictures of us. Normally I didn't make it a practice of explaining shit to a chick, but this time I had no choice.

I rushed to the house and opened the door. The smell of bleach smacked me in the face as soon as I walked through the foyer. Now, I'd heard of people doing a lot of things when they get upset, like exercise, write, go for walk, but this was the first time I'd seen someone go on a cleaning binge then burn pictures. I followed the scent of bleach and burning paper up the stairs to the master bathroom. There I saw my girl sitting at the bathroom window with stacks of my money, pulling off twenty after twenty, setting them on fire, and throwing it out the window.

Without thinking I rushed toward her and grabbed her throat. My first instinct was to set that bitch on fire and throw her ass out the window, but her gasps for air snapped me back to reality.

"Bitch!" I pushed her to the floor and began to gather my money. I grabbed a Gucci duffle and threw my money in there then began to grab some clothes.

Even though this was my house, I wasn't going to stay a second longer; otherwise I was definitely catching a charge tonight.

As I rambled through the closet to pick out a few key pieces of clothing, my girl screamed, "I hate your trifling ass!"

I ain't say shit to her ass as I gathered my things. I just needed to get the fuck out of dodge, and fast.

In five minutes flat, I had my bag packed with enough clothes to last me a week. I glanced around the room one last time before exiting.

My girl lit a blunt and took a pull from it. She said calmly, "Don't forget your shit in the bathroom."

From the look on that bitch face, I could tell she'd done some real fucked-up shit. I tried to think of the worst possible scenarios as I prepared myself to enter the bathroom.

I walked in and glanced around, but didn't notice anything strange. "What the fuck you talking about?" I asked, anxious to get out of the house.

She shot me a devious smirk. "The bathtub."

I took a deep breath as I pulled back the shower curtain. I almost fainted when I looked down. Both of my chinchillas that I'd spent twenty thousand dollars on each were in the tub, soaking in bleach. I could feel my blood pressure rise, the more I looked at them. I ripped the shower curtain down, pulling the rod with it, and stormed out the bathroom.

My girl stood in the middle of the floor, a Kool-Aid smile on her face.

Although everything in me said, "Beat that bitch, stomp that whore, whup that trick," like I was Terrence Howard on *Hustle & Flow*, I used every ounce of strength I had and walked right past her.

"Yeah, that's what you better do—Walk away, you little pussy!"

I stopped in my tracks as my girl's words pierced my ears. "Bitch!" I smacked her, and she fell to the floor. I yelled, "You ain't shit without me!" and proceeded to rip every piece of clothing and jewelry off her. Then I pulled her down the steps, ass naked. "And get the fuck out my house!" I pulled her out the front door and locked it behind me.

Once outside, I hopped in my car, leaving my girl standing in the nude as I pulled off. I sped out of the neighborhood and never looked back. My head was racing as I drove. I didn't know what to think. And the constant ringing of my cell phones was driving me crazy.

I looked at my phone to see who was blowing me up. It was my man Calico. Then it hit me. *Oh shit! I forgot to pay my tab! I know that bitch is tripping too. I did exactly what I told her I wasn't gon' do. Damn!*

I busted a U-turn and headed back in the direction of the bar, where I arrived ten minutes later. I jumped out the car and rushed in.

As soon as I walked through the door, I saw Calico holding Ciara, whispering in her ear. *What the fuck y'all doing?* I thought as I walked up to them.

As soon as Calico noticed me, he said, "Touch, get your baby momma, man."

As I examined the situation before me, I thought to myself, *What the fuck for? It looks like you got her right where you want her, nigga.*

"Trayvon, don't need to do shit," Ciara snapped. "That's why that bitch 'bout to get her ass whupped now . . . because of Trayvon."

I was wondering how so much shit could happen in one night. For a nigga like me, this was unheard of, and I was close to becoming undone. No one wants to see when that happens. "What the fuck is going on?"

"Man, she tripping on ol' girl," Calico said.

I looked over at Diana standing at the bar getting some drinks, oblivious to what was going on. I shook my head and pulled out a hundred dollars. "Pay my tab for me, man." I handed the money to Calico. "And you"—I grabbed Ciara—"let's go."

Ciara looked over her shoulder first at Calico then gave Diana an evil glare and grabbed my hand and came without hesitation. I wasn't sure what that eye contact with Calico was about, but I was sure gon' find out later. I didn't trust Ciara one bit, but I was more irritated because I didn't want Diana caught up in no bullshit because of me. I knew how Ciara and her girls could get, and I didn't even want Diana caught up in that.

I was drained as hell as I drove all the way to Chesapeake to take Ciara home. I was glad when I got to her crib. I didn't even park, I just pulled up in front and hit the unlock button, a sign for her to get the fuck out.

"Damn, you ain't even gon' come and see your kids," Ciara spat.

"Don't even come at me like I'm some deadbeat dad. They should be 'sleep anyway."

"So what?" She yelled as though I was around the block somewhere and not right in her face.

I wouldn't mind seeing my lil' fat rats, I thought. I swung the car around in a parking spot and hopped out. Then I followed Ciara to her apartment.

As soon as she put the key in the door, I could hear the twins.

"Mommy's home!" they yelled. They ran and hugged Ciara as she stepped through the door. "Hey, Mommy."

Kennedy was the first to see me. She yelled, "Dad-dddyyyy!" and rushed over and hugged me tight.

I picked her and Reagan both up in my arms and kissed them. "What y'all still doing up?" I said as I sat on the couch.

"Watching this damn Beyoncé DVD," their aunt said, sounding exhausted. She'd been watching them all day while Ciara ran the streets.

"A'ight, girls, time for bed." I held my hands out for each of them to grab one.

As we walked to their room, Reagan said, "Can you read us a bedtime story?"

"Yep. What y'all want me to read?"

"*Dora*," they both said in unison.

"*Dora*? Nah, she a punk," I said to tease the girls. "What about Diego?"

Kennedy said right away, "Daddy, Diego is for boys. We are girls."

"A'ight, a'ight. *Dora the Explorer*, it is."

Once I got the girls tucked in and started to read Dora, they fell fast asleep. I looked at the time. It was already three A.M. Since I was comfortable, I decided to get in a quick nap.

Three minutes after I closed my eyes, Ciara yelled, "Trayvon! Trayvon, wake up!"

"Yeah?" I wondered what the fuck she wanted.

"Come get in the bed," she said, grabbing my hand.

I looked at the girls, who were both out for the count. I

got up and kissed them on the cheeks then headed to Ciara's room. I pulled off everything, except my boxers, and lay down, and she slid in beside me.

Just as I was dozing off to sleep, I felt a hand glide against my dick. I turned on my back and looked over my right shoulder at Ciara. She was ass naked.

Although my dick was saying yes, my mind was saying fuck no! There was no way I could fuck Ciara. She was already a crazy baby momma. If I fucked her, the bitch would really lose her mind. In her mind, that would mean we were getting back together, and no way in hell was that ever happening.

"Come on, chill with that bullshit, Ciara."

"So you trying to tell me you gon' lay up in here next to me and not fuck me, Trayvon?"

"Basically." I rolled back over on my side, putting my back to her.

"Well, then get out." Ciara shoved me with her foot, forcing me off the bed.

I wasn't up for another argument or fight, so I put my shit on and broke out. There was no way I was going back to my house. I figured my girl had probably called the police and everything, so when I got in the car, I hit Jewel up.

"Hello?" Jewel said in one of those deep-ass sleep voices.

"Damn, you sound like a man. I'm homeless," I said, knowing she would offer her place.

"Come through, Touch. You know where the key is." Jewel then hung up the phone.

I looked up at the sky as I drove to her house. *It's gotta be a full moon*, I thought, recalling the crazy night I'd had.

Fifteen minutes later, I was at Jewel's crib, knocked out in her guest bedroom. Finally, I had the opportunity to let my guard down and get some much-needed rest.

* * *

"Damn." I woke to the smell of bacon and a growling stomach.

I drug myself out of the bed and into the bathroom. As I stood in front of the toilet to take a piss, I looked down at my hard dick and wished I had some hot, wet, morning pussy to push it in. For a moment, I actually fantasized about ramming my dick up in Jewel. I quickly shook that from my head, flushed the toilet, and washed up before following the smell of bacon into the kitchen.

I walked up on Jewel as she chatted away on the phone. "You made enough for me, yo?"

"You the only reason I'm cooking, nigga," Jewel responded as she poured the blueberry waffle mix into the waffle maker. "I don't do breakfast."

"Damn, man! You always got that phone glued to your ear. Ain't you afraid of getting ear cancer or some shit?"

We both laughed at the thought, and I grabbed a seat at the breakfast bar. I listened to Jewel talk on the phone as I waited for her to finish cooking.

I heard her say into the phone, "What? Please don't trip. That is Touch. I told you we were tight. He's like my brother."

I wondered who the fuck she was talking to. It seemed like we had to go through this same shit with every nigga she fucked with. Every single one of those cats assumed me and Jewel had something other than a friendship.

"Okay, I'll call you later." Jewel hung up the phone.

"Who was that?" I asked, my face balled-up.

She smirked. "Your crazy-ass friend?"

"Who?" I wondered who the fuck she could be talking about.

"Calico."

"Calico? Are you serious?" I asked, hoping she was joking.

"Yes, Calico."

"I just saw this nigga last night. He ain't even say shit about y'all kicking it."

"Yeah. We were together all day yesterday. We went shopping and everything. Which reminds me, I got the girls something."

"And that nigga already tripping?"

"Nah, he was saying to call him when I was free," Jewel said, already making excuses for him, "and he didn't know we were close like that to be spending the night together."

"Yo, give me the phone and let me call that nigga." I reached for the house phone.

"Ahh . . . no. Me and him ain't even like that for him to be trying to trip, so don't waste your time." Jewel grabbed the cordless phone and pushed it out of my reach. "So what the hell happen last night?" she asked as she made my plate.

"To make a long story short, my baby momma fucked with ol' girl again, and the bitch went crazy. When I went home, the bitch had bleached my furs and was burning my money. So I released her from all the shit I bought, which left her naked, and I pitched her dumb ass out my house. I went back to the bar where Ciara was beefing with a chick I was hollering at earlier in the night. So I grabbed her and took her home. My fat rats were awake, so I chilled with them and ended up falling asleep in their bed and shit. Ciara wakes me up and tells me to go get in her bed. Then the bitch wants to fuck. Now you know the worse thing I could possibly do is fuck her, so I refused. Now she starts to trip, so I dip out on her. I thought the other bitch might have called the cops, so thinking the block was hot, I called you for a place to crash, and here I am."

"Damn, Touch, you had a busy night. You're always gettin' into shit because of your baby mother. Why don't you check her on that crazy shit she be doing?" Jewel asked as she placed my plate in front of me.

"Ain't no talking to that girl, Jewel."

"Whatever." Jewel passed me a glass of orange juice. "Deep inside, I think you don't want her to leave you alone. You like the fact that she be going crazy over your ass."

"Nah, man. I can't stand the drama."

"So why y'all ain't together anyway? You never really told me the whole story, you know."

"She fucked up," I said, trying not to really go into details. "I could never trust that bitch again."

Jewel really started digging deep into my business and inquired more, just like I knew she would. "What did she do?"

The truth was, that shit Ciara did really fucked me up. And that shit her and Calico was doing the night before was kind of suspect. It took me back to that shit she'd done before. A nigga was hurt and I hated reliving that moment. But I'd never kept anything from Jewel for this long, so I thought I'd come out with it.

"When I was locked up, she started fucking one of my little worker cats, a nigga I put on the corner."

"What? Are you serious?"

"Yeah. A lil' nothing-ass nickel-and-dime cat." I shook my head.

"I can tell that shit really hurt you, Touch." Jewel stared me in my face, seemingly waiting for a reaction.

"Look, I ain't never lied to you before, and I'm not gon' start now. My baby mother is the only chick I've ever loved," I said, confessing my feelings for Ciara for the first time, "so you damn straight—That shit fucked me up, when I found out she fucked my man. But, you know, it is what it is."

"I know you still love her, and I know you love your twins, so why don't you just be with her and have one big happy family?" Jewel said it like it was an easy fix.

"Can't do it. I don't go back."

"Nah. You just got too much pride. You know niggas would clown you." Jewel's words were painfully true.

"You might be right."

"I know I am. Just try it. You don't have to dive into it headfirst. Shit, what do you have to lose? I know you ain't trying to get back with ol' girl. She probably ain't even trying to fuck with you like that anymore, anyway. So why not holler at your baby mother?"

I let what Jewel said go in one ear and leave out the other. "We'll see."

"Well, can we see my truck?" Jewel said, reminding me that I still hadn't brought her truck back to the crib.

"Oh shit. It's at my mom's house in the garage. We can go get it after breakfast."

"That's cool. I need to holler at Ma Dukes anyway."

"Yo, I told you about that shit."

My mother loved Jewel like she was the daughter she never had. For some reason, they clicked from the first day they'd met. Every time my mother would see or speak to Jewel, the first thing I'd hear was, "I really like her, Trayvon, I really do."

"Don't hate because Ma loves me!" Jewel cleared the bar then walked into her bedroom. "Momma knows best, baby boy. Momma knows best."

You might be right. I reached for a cigarette then massaged my rising dick as I watched the silhouette of Jewel's ass bounce beneath her satin robe.

Chapter 5

"One Love Out and Another One In"

Jewel

A week or so had gone and, for the most part, my life as I knew was pretty quiet. That silence was interrupted by a familiar ringtone.

"It's your baby. Pick up. It's your baby. Pick up," the voice from my cell constantly repeated.

I sat up in the bed and rubbed my eyes as I tried to figure out where my phone was. I finally found it on the dressing table and quickly flipped it open. "Hello?" I said through a cracked voice.

"Hi, Jewel," Sasha said faintly.

"What's up, Sasha? How are you doing?"

"Not too good. I miss you, Jewel. I'm leaving today, and there was no way I could leave without seeing you."

"Damn."

Reality had finally set in. It wasn't until that point that I realized how much Sasha really meant to me. True, she irritated me at times with her constant nagging and the poor decisions she made, but she was still my boobie and I loved her.

"So that's all you have to say?" Sasha asked.

"No. Actually, I don't know what to say. This is all of a sudden."

"Well, I already did a quick sale on my house, sold my car to a used-car dealer, turned off all my utilities, and broke up with Rick."

"Well, at least one good thing came out of all this," I said, referring to her breakup. "So what's next? You just gonna live in Georgia now?"

"I'm gonna stay with my mom, and dance in Atlanta. Hopefully, I'll get my money right and be able to get back on my feet."

I tried to give some encouraging words. "Sounds like a plan. Sometimes you just gotta start over, in a fresh environment, you know what I mean?"

"Yeah, I feel ya. So what do I have to do to get me a baller when I hit the *A*?"

"Oh, now you want advice from the gold-digging whore," I said in a joking tone.

"Jewel! You know you're not a whore. I'm sorry for anything I may have said the last time when we spoke. I was angry and jealous about the whole situation."

"Apology accepted," I said, with no hesitation.

"I swear, that's why I love you so much. You have the biggest heart in the world! *Muah!*" Sasha kissed the phone.

"Kisses back at you, Boobie."

"Okay, now to business. Tell me how to get my rich man!" For once Sasha seemed really interested in my advice.

"All right, listen carefully. Matter of fact, you might need to jot this down." I laughed then continued. "First, you have to look, act, and talk like a top-notch chick. Your persona can't say stripper, groupie, or gold digger. Show that you are pretty and intelligent, not some dumb chick. You should familiarize yourself with upscale places in the area.

"Next, you have to know your target. You have to be able to identify real money; know the difference between dope boy money versus athlete, entertainment, and distinguished money. Don't be fooled by exotic car rentals, fake jewelry, and fake clothes. Men with genuine money are reserved and on the low. They have nothing to prove, and therefore they're not flamboyant, and never seeking attention.

"Once you've identified your man, you have to get his attention. Do this by sending him and his boys a drink. On your first date, pull out your wallet and prepare to pay. Although he will stop you, he will find it very impressive. If things go farther, when you're out shopping, bring him back something significant, like his favorite cologne. When you're spending the night at his house, tidy up a little, and more importantly, get up and go to work in the morning.

"Now this is the part where most women fuck up, so pay close attention. Play your position. I repeat—Play your position. Know that you are more than likely not the only female in his life. Nine times out of ten, he has a wife at home, which makes you a mistress. Never compete with the home front. Don't smother him. You will receive monetary support and gifts for the lack of attention. And, last but not least, satisfy your man sexually. Have a huge sexual appetite, learn what turns him on and off, and be prepared to fill his every fantasy. You want to do everything that his wife or the next girl won't do. So if that means threesomes, sucking dick, licking ass or fucking in the ass, be prepared and willing to do it." I ran down the dos and don'ts like I wrote the manual.

"Damn, it's that serious, huh? I think I got it, though. I'm gonna put it to the test in Atlanta. I'll let you know if it works."

"It's foolproof, baby," I assured her. "I promise you, if executed correctly, it will work."

"Oh, I know. If anybody knows how to get a man or woman, it's you. Hell, you even got the power to get straight bitches." Sasha somehow managed to turn this conversation around to talk about Shakira.

"Blah, blah, blah, blah," I sang to cut her off. "I'm not trying to hear that shit. This is your last day here. You supposed to be over here fucking me like you will never get another piece of pussy in life." I knew that would grab her attention.

"That's why I was calling. I want to spend my last hours with you. Are you going to come get me?"

"Is everything in order?" I asked, to be sure she had mended all her loose ends.

"Yep. They closed on the house today. The family I sold the furniture to came and got the last of it yesterday. I dropped off my truck this morning, and the boys have already made it to Georgia." Sasha ran down everything to me.

"Okay, I'm on my way." I hung up the phone, freshened up, and headed out the door.

Thirty minutes later, I was in front of her house. Sasha hopped in, and I put the truck in drive to pull off.

"Wait." Sasha placed her hand on top of mine at the gearshift.

I put the truck back in park. "What's wrong?"

Sasha didn't respond. She just stared at her house.

"Did you forget something?" I asked, confused by her actions.

Again she didn't say anything, but she did shake her head no. I had a feeling that something was really wrong. I gently grabbed her by her chin and turned her toward me. And, just as I'd thought, tears were rolling down her eyes. I didn't say a word. I just grabbed her and hugged her tight. I listened as she cried hysterically.

"This is my house, Jewel," she said, forcing out the words. "This is all I had left. Now I have nothing, absolutely nothing. No car, no furniture, no home, nothing. All I have is a shitload of dance costumes and heels, and a single suitcase of daily clothes."

Damn, I thought to myself, *she doesn't deserve this*. I truly felt bad for her.

"Baby, I wish I could make it all right," I told her. "Look, before you know it, things will be better. Just go to Atlanta and stack your dough. When you get a little saved up, I'll put it in the right places and make things happen."

"Okay, baby." Sasha wiped her tears away, and I pulled off.

It wasn't until I got home that I realized I was really gonna miss Sasha.

The next couple of hours were spent in pure ecstasy. Sasha had made me feel things I'd never felt before and in places I've never felt before. I'd never felt such pleasure in my life. She definitely left her mark.

As she was washing up to prepare to leave, I went through my dresser drawers and my closet and collected things I knew she would like. When she came out the bathroom, I had a number of jeans, dresses, shirts and bags waiting for her.

"Too bad you don't wear my shoe size," I said as she looked as the things I had laid out for her.

"This is for me?" Sasha said in disbelief.

"Yes. I want you to have them."

"Your True Religion, Joe's Jeans, and Rock and Republic? They still have tags on them!" Sasha said, still in doubt.

"Baby, it's all yours," I reassured her.

"Even your Prada bag?"

"Everything on the bed, Boobie."

"Damn!" Sasha rushed over and kissed me passionately. "I love you so much!"

"I want it back when you come back to VA, though." I shot her a quick look. "I'm just joking."

We laughed together.

The trip to the airport and the good-byes were heart-wrenching. I drove home depressed like a little girl who'd just lost her puppy. I turned on the TV and flipped through the channels as my mind wandered. I thought about all the good times and all the bad times we'd shared. I never thought I would miss her as much as I did.

My house phone began to ring, interrupting my reminiscing.

"Hello," I said without even looking at the caller ID.

A male voice said, "May I speak with Mrs. Burroughs, please?"

"You have the wrong number," I said and prepared to hang up.

"I believe I have the correct number," the person said on the other end of the phone.

The voice began to sound familiar to me.

"Who is this?" I asked

"Mr. Burroughs," he responded.

"Calico?" I said, figuring it could only be him.

"What up? How you gon' be my wifey and not know your last name?"

I snapped, "You never offered to give me your government name. I figured you would tell me when you wanted me to know."

"Michael Burroughs. You happy?"

"Nah. I need a social security number, permanent address, and the name and phone number of your nearest relative," I spat back.

"Damn. What am I doing, applying for a line of credit?" Calico laughed.

"I'm just fucking with you. So when am I going to see you? I'm real lonely right now."

"I'll be there probably in a week or so."

"What if I can't wait that long?" I said, just to see how he would respond.

"Then I'll come sooner."

"Yeah, right," I said, knowing he was just talking shit.

"I'm serious. I'll do whatever makes you happy."

"Well, in that case, can you make everything right so my girl can come back to Virginia?" I said, really missing Sasha.

"Huh?" Calico was thrown by my request.

"My girl Sasha just left to go to Georgia. She had to move because shit was really fucked-up for her here. So she's going down there for a while to try and get things back in order. She just left, and I already miss her."

"I'm sorry, baby. I wish I was there to pamper you. You want me to catch a flight tomorrow?" Calico asked.

"Are you serious?"

"Yeah, but you can't let nobody know I'm coming. Niggas gon' expect this to be a business trip, and my phone gonna be blowing up the entire time. I'll have to hide out at your crib or something, and we won't be able to hang out."

"First of all, no one sleeps in my bed except rent-paying tenants. And, lastly, what fun would that be if we have to be cramped up in the crib anyway? I'll rather wait."

"That's cool. We can wait. I was just trying to be there for you. And, for the record, I don't mind paying rent. How much is it?" Calico asked like it was nothing.

"My mortgage"—I put emphasis on the word *mortgage*—"is twelve hundred a month."

"A'ight, I got you. Do I need to put down a deposit too?" Calico said, cool as a fan.

"I don't know. Maybe I should ask for a deposit, since you refused to supply information to put in a credit application." I giggled.

"I ain't got no problem putting down a deposit. So when is my move in date?"

"We'll discuss that when the funds have been secured. I accept cash only, Mr. Burroughs." I spoke to him in a professional tone as though I was a property manager.

"Okay, well, I guess we've got a contracted lease. You can pick your funds up at a Western Union in about an hour."

"Okay. Bye"

"Gone." Calico ended the call.

I watched the clock constantly as I counted down the minutes. After about forty-five minutes, I couldn't wait any longer. I hopped in my truck and headed to the grocery store to check on the wire. I filled out the Western Union form and gave the cashier my ID.

"Do you know how much?" she asked.

Now my first thought was to say, "Did I put in an amount on the form?" Instead I chose to be nice and replied, "No, I don't."

The cashier huffed and puffed as she entered the information in the computer. "Do you have the money transfer control number?"

Now this time I just had to respond, "Do you see one on the paper?"

The cashier must have gone with her better judgment and decided to keep any comments after that to herself. She handed me the money order and directed me to sign at the X.

I glanced at the amount. "Three thousand, umph," I said to no one in particular.

The cashier counted out my money, and I pranced out the store with a big smile on my face.

I called Calico as soon as I reached my truck. "Okay, it looks like I have a new tenant. When would you like to move in?" I asked as soon as he answered, pretending to be a landlord.

Calico played along. "When will the place be ready?"

"Immediately," I responded, wanting him to come right away.

Calico laughed at my eagerness.

I figured, since we'd touched the money subject, this would be a good time to talk about exactly what type of business Calico had. Deep inside I already knew the deal, but I wanted to see just how he would carry it. I wanted to know if he was gonna be up front with me or keep playing the "I'm-a-businessman" game.

"Do you remember the first time you saw me?"

"Of course, I do," he answered confidently.

I knew he thought I was referring to the bar, so I figured I would use this as an opportunity to get a little deeper in his pockets. "I bet you don't."

"I'm a gambling man, so I'm game. Set your wager." Calico was enthusiastic about our little competition.

"Okay. If you win, I'll give one sexual pleasure of my choice. If I win, you have to take me to Potomac Mills Outlet for a day of shopping." I said, laying down the rules.

"That's cool with me. I just hope you can keep up your end of the bargain," Calico said as though he knew he was going to win the bet.

"Okay, so what's the answer?"

"It was a Friday," Calico began to say very carefully. "The day I saw you at the bar with Touch."

"Wrong!" I said right away, interrupting him. "So when are we going shopping?"

"Damn, you ain't even let me finish."

"No need, hon. You are wrong. Now the answer to my question, please."

"As soon as I get there," Calico responded, no longer putting up a fight.

"Okay, and I'm holding you to this too."

"No problem."

"Why you so quick to give money up?" I asked, directing the conversation to where I really wanted it to go.

"What make you say that?"

"Well, you took me shopping on our first date. You sent me three grand like it was nothing, and now you just agreed to take me shopping again with no problem. The average dude ain't coming off no money like that, especially with a chick he's only known for a couple of days."

Calico gave the safest answer he could, but that wasn't gonna stop me from finding out what I wanted to know. "I feel like I've known you for years."

"I'm sure, but that doesn't answer my question. I've noticed you're pretty good at avoiding subjects that you rather not talk about, but in order for this thing we have to go any further, I have to know exactly who I am dealing with."

I heard him chuckle on the other end of the phone. "I like you, Jewel, but there are things that I can't tell you. Not yet anyway. I am good at dodging bullets and questions. It comes with the territory. I do this for a reason, and I shouldn't have to defend that at all."

I listened as Calico talked. I heard what he was selling, but I wasn't sure if I was buying. Calico had so much game, it was almost impossible to tell when he was lying from when he was being sincere.

"When you're in my position, it puts even the ones you care about at risk. That's why I do my business on the East Coast. When I was working in the area where I lay my head, at shit got too hot. I'm constantly worrying about the safety of my kids and their mothers as well as the rest of my family. Withholding shit from friends and relatives in my line of business keeps niggas breathing for at least another day."

I wondered what type of girl he figured I was. "So what are you saying, Calico?"

"You ain't ready for all the shit that goes down in my line of work. You ain't no 'ride-or-die' chick. You ain't that chick that can sit through interrogation and not rat. You're not that chick that can go deliver a package or hold shit down if I get locked up. I mean, would you even know how to bail a nigga out?"

Calico's words cut me deep. If any other nigga would have said this to me, they would have certainly found themselves alone, but his words, however harsh, were true.

Although I had a gold-digger's eye and could easily categorize a man based on his wealth, I had never been "a gangster's girl." Frankly, because dope-boy money had never been long enough for a bitch like me, but I wasn't gon' let this nigga know that. Something about Calico was different from those cats, particularly because he was the nigga giving out the orders and not taking them. But, besides that, I think I was really starting to like him.

I didn't want him to know that his words affected me in the least, so I did what any bitch would. I put on a front.

"You've just proven I am good at what I do. Don't let the image fool you. That's why I'm never suspect, because even though I know the game inside and out, I look like 'miss corporate America,' " I lied.

"That's hard to believe, but I'm not the one to call anybody a liar. Trust me, time will tell."

"It sure will."

"It's more to it than just standing by your man side though. You gotta always be on point. You can't be distracted by any nigga that pass you in a shopping center in a drop-top

Benz. I bet you know how many karats were in my ear," Calico said, proving he did know the first time he saw me.

"You tricked me!" I yelled, shocked that he really remembered that first glance.

"No, I didn't. You cut me off. You were too eager. You moved too fast. That could fuck you up in the game. But a real ride-or-die chick would know that, right?" Calico tried to make a point.

"Whatever! Finish what you were saying."

"All I got a chance to say is, it was a Friday, the day I saw you at the bar. If you would have let me finished, I would have continued by saying, you passed me as you chatted away on your cell phone going downtown, probably on your way to the nail shop."

"And how do you know I was on my way to the nail shop?"

"Observation, another skill that comes with the territory."

"Okay, okay! Maybe I'm not 'married to the game,' but I can be that chick by your side, and I'm not afraid to prove it."

"Action speaks louder than words. Don't talk about it, be about it."

On that note I was ready to end the call. "Enough said."

Chapter 6

"Juggling Chicks"

Touch

*D*amn, I ain't even trying to see this bitch, I thought as I rounded the corner, heading toward my crib. I had been chilling at Ciara's crib for the last week and a half, so I wouldn't have to kill a bitch, but since I had run out of clothes, I had to come back. Although I thought it was gonna be hell staying with Ciara, shit turned out all right. We had a few arguments, but all in all, it was cool being around my girls. For a split second, I actually thought about really getting back with her, but that shit flew out the window as soon as it entered my mind.

"Yes, sir!" I said to myself as I put the car in park and jumped out.

The house was empty. Everything was in the same order that it was left that night I fought with ol' girl. Tired of her constant bullshit, I packed her shit and told her to come through for it. She was trying to act different on the phone, being all calm and cute, telling me that she'll be by in twenty minutes. While I waited, I tried to straighten up.

When she got to the house, she pleaded with me to forgive her, but like I said once before, I don't go back. She finally realized my mindset when she found her stuff in two plastic garbage bags. I told her that I had something to do, so we needed to make this quick.

She flipped out. "Where you in a rush to? You still running after your baby momma, huh? Well, she can have your sorry ass then!"

"Bitch, whatever," I said. Truth be told, this was a good move for me. I never even clicked with her like that anyway.

"I was a good fucking girl to you," she yelled as she was reaching for her car door.

"Nah, what you lost was a good man. What's sad, you don't know shit about me." Me and ol' girl were together for a good minute now. You would think she would know how I flex and that I wouldn't even roll with my baby mother like that. This bitch ain't even know my drink! I thought about what Jewel said and decided to put her to the test.

"What color are my eyes?"

"What? What kind of fucking question is that?"

I gave her another chance to answer. "What color are my eyes?"

I faintly heard, "I don't fucking know," and she got in the car and then quickly sped off.

Exactly! Eat dust, bitch. I looked at her from my door, confident that I'd made the right decision. I took her two garbage bags full of stuff to the curb and then went back into the house.

After about an hour of flipping TV channels, I realized I hadn't talked to my road dawg in a while, so I pulled out my cell phone to hit Jewel up.

"I was just about to call you," Jewel said as soon as she picked up.

"Oh yeah? So what was stopping you?"

"Whatever! Where the fuck you been? Boo'd up somewhere?" Jewel snapped.

"Chill out, man. I been at my baby mother crib."

"Ah shit now! You been doing the family thing. I'm cool with that. I told you, you need to get back with that girl anyway."

"I don't know about that shit. I can't lie, shit was cool when I was there. She made sure a nigga ate. I had my fat rats around me all the time. I had to admit, that shit was a'ight."

"Well, I'm glad to hear that. I just want you to find you someone and settle down. You're a good guy, and you deserve a good girl."

"You know I ain't even that nigga that got a bunch of bitches. I do my thang, but I don't mind having a steady bitch. You know me, I do the relationship thing," I told her.

"Yeah, I know, but you just be picking the wrong damn chicks."

"Yeah, yeah, yeah." I wasn't trying to hear that shit Jewel was talking. "I'm gonna need you to take me to the airport next week. I'm going to the *A*."

"Okay, I got you. But, anyway, on to me, I talked to your boy today."

"Yeah? What that nigga talking 'bout?"

"Well, I think I really like him. He sent me three grand today," Jewel said full of excitement.

Oh shit. This nigga 'bout to pull one on Jewel, I said to myself. I knew exactly how Calico moved. He was known for running game on bitches and giving them money and gifts and shit to win them over then convincing them to let him chill at their crib, and the next thing you know, he doing work out their crib and have them doing runs for him. But I was hoping that Jewel was smarter than that.

"So what's three grand, Jewel? That ain't no money, and

you for one should know that," I said, wondering if my homegirl was slipping.

"I know that, Touch. Of course, I've gotten much more than that from dudes, but the difference is, I ain't even known him that long, and I ain't put in no work. This nigga took me shopping and sent me three grand in this little bit of time. Plus, this is dope boy money, not entertainer or athlete money that I'm normally dealing with."

As I listened to Jewel speak, I thought, *Damn, he told the truth about what he does.*

"Touch, you hear me?" Jewel asked in reaction to my lack of response.

"Whatever you say, lil' homie," I said, uneasy about the whole situation.

"I need to know some things, though."

"What's up?"

"Does Calico have a chick here?"

"Come on, Jewel. You know I'm not into shit like this. You not 'bout to turn me into Mr. Palmer," I said, referring to this Jamaican cat around here. He would call the cops in a moment's notice if he saw you hanging out on the corner two seconds longer than you should be. For business, he was a real pain in the ass.

"So it's like that, Touch. This nigga is going to be staying with me when he come here, so I need know what the deal is."

My fucking stomach sank when she said that. *I can't believe this fucking chick. Has she lost her fucking mind? This ain't even her. She on some bullshit right now.*

"Jewel, what are you doing? I thought you were smarter than this. You don't even know this nigga."

"I actually know a whole lot about him. We've had extensive phone conversations."

"A'ight den. If you know so much, you don't need to be asking me shit. You on your own with this one. You're a smart girl, you know the game. Hell, you run game. And game always recognize game, right?" I left it at that.

"Fa sho!" Jewel yelled back, and we ended the call soon after.

My dick was aching as I drove back to my baby mother's house. I needed some pussy bad, but I wasn't trying to fuck her. That shit was like committing suicide. Ciara was already on some bullshit when I wasn't fucking her, so I could only imagine what would happen if I started. In her mind, that would mean we're back together.

Just then, Diana popped in my head. I wondered if Ciara had fucked things up between the two of us as I took a quick exit off the interstate and headed toward Mo Dean's instead of my original destination.

The parking lot was packed as I pulled up to the restaurant. I circled the block and parked on the street. I figured that probably was best as I walked up. At least, that way if my baby mother or one of her snitch-ass friends passed by, they wouldn't see my car in the parking lot and be tempted to come in and ruin my night.

I scanned the club from the entrance and proceeded with caution, to make sure the crowd was to my liking. I walked in and grabbed a seat at the bar. I ordered my usual as I looked around for Diana. I didn't see her in my immediate area, and hoped that she was just at a booth or something, where I couldn't see her. To waste a little time, I began to play one of the many computerized games that sat in front of me.

Just as I was getting into the game, someone hugged me from behind and whispered in my ear, "Hey, sexy."

My dick rose as though it had ears and recognized the

voice. I turned around to greet Diana. "Dirty Diana," I sang. "What's up, baby?"

"You." She looked at the imprint of my swollen penis in my Five-Four jeans.

I got right to the point. "You gotdamn right. So what you gon' do about that?"

"I'm down. I've been down. You the one with that baby momma drama."

"Baby momma drama?" I played stupid because I knew Diana had no idea what was going on the other night at the club.

"Yeah, baby momma drama. Our boy, Calico, told me all about it."

What? What kind of bitch shit is that? I wondered what type of trouble Calico was trying to start.

"Fuck all dat. Let's do this. Can you leave now?" I wasn't trying to waste no more time talking about bullshit and take the risk of my baby mother blowing my spot up again.

"Right now? I'm working."

I pulled Diana between my legs and grabbed a handful of her ass cheeks with each one of my hands. "He want you right now," I whispered in her ear as I pressed my manhood against her thigh.

"Well"—She paused as she glanced around the restaurant—"it's slow, so I guess so." She untied her waitress apron and headed to the back of the bar to notify them she was leaving.

As we hopped in the car, my mind was spinning about where I could take her and not run into anyone else. I thought about the dope house, but it was just too many niggas at that crib. I needed to find a spot fast. My dick was rock-hard, and I needed to bust a nut before I caught a bad case of blue balls.

"My electric bill is due. I'm gonna need something," Diana whispered in my ear, while rubbing on my dick.

Spoken like a typical chickenhead. *No wonder this bitch was throwing the pussy at a nigga. She out for money. It is what it is. At this point I don't even give a fuck. I don't mind a jump-off. It ain't like a nigga trying to wife her*, I thought to myself but decided against voicing it.

Temples sweating, I answered, "A'ight, I got you." I pulled out a hundred-dollar bill.

Normally, I would only throw a jump-off sixty or seventy dollars, but at the time, I was thinking with my dick instead of my mind.

Shortly after, we passed a Roadway Inn, hiding off to the side near Shore Drive. *Perfect.* I busted a U-turn and headed into the parking lot and parked. Diana stayed in the car while I checked in.

Minutes later, she was following me to room number 208.

"What you want? What you want to do?" she asked with a slight attitude, pulling off her clothes as if she was going to bed. She didn't even try to undress in a sexy way to keep me turned on. It seemed like Diana had the same intentions as me, fucking and bucking.

"It don't matter, but first, a nigga need to piss." I headed for the bathroom, unbuckling my pants.

A minute later, Diana was standing at the bathroom door ass-naked with one hand on her hip. She looked at her watch on the other. "Hurry up. I got some things to take care of. For a hundred dollars, you can't get much," she said like the trick she was.

"Soon as I bust, we can go," I answered. I shook the last few drops off my dick then grabbed some tissue to wipe my tip.

I walked into the room and sat on the edge of the bed and

signaled Diana to come over. Then, I pulled her head down to my dick. Bobbing her head up and down, Diana was beginning to choke, but I didn't give a fuck. Plus, I didn't like her nasty attitude. This bitch acted like she was into a nigga, but all she really was into was a nigga's pockets.

But what I did like was the way this bitch sucked the skin off my dick and was playing with my balls at the same time. A service like that deserved payment.

"Ah fuck! Suck that dick, bitch!"

Diana stopped her dick-sucking duty for a brief moment. "I don't swallow, and you get one more position, nigga."

Damn, this bitch is a trick for real! The realization sat in as I registered her last statement. *Well, better make the best of this, since I'm officially a john.* "Yeah, a'ight."

I picked Diana up and both of us landed on the dresser against the mirror. Her legs were wide open while she played with her pussy. I quickly put on a condom. One thing for sure was, I didn't need any more fat rats running around, and definitely didn't need a trick-ass baby mother, or even worse, that monster that a nigga can't shake.

After placing my dick into Diana's wet pussy, I began choking her. I decided to use this as an opportunity to do that rough-sex shit. To my surprise, this crazy bitch loved it.

"Choke me harder, nigga," she screamed.

"You want it harder, bitch?"

"Yes, choke me. Fuck me. Give it to me real hard! Fuck this pussy up!"

The look of excitement and fear, plus her extremely wet pussy, made me come within minutes.

Damn, I needed that, I thought as she got up to shower.

I reached for a washcloth to wash off my dick. *That was the best hundred dollars I ever spent*. I pulled out a cigarette.

By the time I finished smoking, Diana was out the shower, and we were headed back to Mo Dean's.

I didn't even bother pulling into the parking lot as I pulled up. I just stopped at the corner and hit the unlock switch and signaled for her to get out. As soon as she closed the door behind her, I pulled off and headed to my crib.

I jumped out the car and headed in the house. I rushed upstairs and started a hot shower. After bathing, I opened the drawer to get toothpaste and toothbrush to finish my hygiene session for the night.

Today was a good day, more or less. I finally got some ass, for a hundred dollars, and there was no baby momma drama. "Finally, a nigga can get a good night sleep," I said aloud to myself.

Chapter 7

"Saved by *C*"

Sasha

"Come back home!" Jewel yelled as soon as she picked up the phone.

"Girl, you're crazy! I ain't even been gone but three days!" I laughed.

"I know, but I miss you already. So how's everything?"

"Well, I'm pretty much settled. I dropped my oldest boy off at his dad's house, and me and the youngest are comfortable here at my parents' house in Columbus. Girl, why this nigga have a big-ass five-bedroom house on a finished basement! He making major bread, and I'm up here struggling! That's some bullshit!"

"Don't worry about what he has. That's motivation for you to get your own shit together. Then you don't have to ask a nigga for nothing! You have your own and anything a dude wants to contribute is extra! Understand?" Jewel quickly shared some real knowledge with me.

"I feel you," I replied. "I checked out a few strip clubs in Atlanta, and I think I found one I want to work at. It's called

Bottoms Up. They have one chick there by the name of Juicy that is supposed to be like the star chick. She got a nice body or whatever, but she doesn't really do any shit that's so amazing to me. I don't feel like it's any real competition there, and the club stays pack. I figure I'll be able to stack dough and get back on my feet in no time."

"Good! It sounds like a plan to me!" Jewel said.

"You know I've even thought 'bout moving out here. I noticed they are doing a lot of building up in Atlanta and the houses are dirt cheap. Plus, it would be good for me to be close to my baby father and parents."

"You know I don't want you away from me. But what you saying is true. Just do what's best for you and your family, baby. Hell, it's a flight from Norfolk to Atlanta daily." Jewel tried to make the best of the situation.

"Well, let me get off this phone. I need to go get my business license and go talk to the manager about a job at the club."

"A'ight. While you at it, why don't you register with a staffing service." Jewel always made me feel like I wasn't doing enough. "It wouldn't be a bad idea to have a job as well, especially if you plan on buying another house or getting a car."

"Okay. I'll talk to you later." I rolled my eyes then ended the call.

I rushed in the bathroom and hopped in the shower and threw on some clothes. I had an hour drive to Atlanta and wanted to miss the traffic.

By noon I'd already gotten my business license and was on my way to the staffing service.

The redhead lady called from the back, "Sasha Lewis."

"Yes?" I stood to my feet and headed in her direction.

We shook hands as she introduced herself and directed me to follow her to the back. She reviewed my resume.

"Oh, you have so much experience in the healthcare field. It shouldn't be hard for you to find a job. I noticed you listed you were interested in medical front office jobs, but it says here you went to school for medical assisting. Why not pursue that route? You could make more much more money."

"Well, I am not certified. I let my certification expire," I said shamefully.

"Oh my! How could you do that?"

Well, if you must know, I was shaking my ass making ten dollars every three minutes, so at the time ten dollars an hour was nothing to me. I told her, "I was in school working towards another career."

"Oh, I see. Well, it's neither here or there. You have a great amount of experience, so I'm sure we can get you a position. You will be hearing from us soon."

"Thank you very much." I shook her hand once more then left the office.

I rushed to my mom's car that I'd borrowed and headed to the strip club. That was my final stop for the day.

I pulled up at Bottoms Up. It was only three in the afternoon, and there was already a small crowd at the club.

I walked up to the security and explained to them I was there to seek employment. They escorted me to the front door and told me to ask for Chastity. I walked to the bar and asked for her.

Moments later, a medium-height, well-dressed, light-skinned female walked out. "How are you?" She held out her hand as she looked me over quickly.

"I'm just fine."

"You can follow me," she said, and we walked toward her office.

I felt comfortable as I walked in. This was unlike any other interview I'd had for a strip club. Chastity was so welcoming, and her office was a professional setting. Unlike the usual let-me-see-you-naked interviews I've had with perverted club owners in the past. Maybe the mere fact that Chastity was a woman alone made me feel better.

"Please have a seat." Chastity handed me a clipboard with a pen and application attached.

Wow! An application? Never did this for a strip club before. I began to fill out the application wondering if I should give my real information. Giving false information was what kept me out of jail when I had my last strip club situation. A chick couldn't press charges if she didn't know a name. This bitch, Chastity, looked like she was about her shit though, so I figured, I'd better go with the real.

After I was done I handed it to her.

"Identification and social security card please." Chastity waited as I shuffled though my new Prada bag I'd received from Jewel.

I handed her my cards, and she went over to the copy machine and made copies. She handed them back to me then sat in her oversized leather chair behind her huge wooden desk.

"So you're from Virginia, Sasha?"

"Yes, I am. I just moved here last week."

"I'm from Virginia myself. I have quite a few friends back home. It says here you danced at Purple Rain. I believe one of my friends use to dance there too. Do you know anyone by the name of Ceazia?"

My heart skipped a beat at the sound of her name. Before Jewel, Ceazia was my world. From the first day we met in the strip club she took me under her wing. We once shared that "little sister-big sister" relationship that Jewel swore she and Paradise had, but it turned to something more. Just like Paradise, I'd never been with a woman, but Ceazia changed all of that for me. She was my first and would always hold a spot in my heart.

"Yes, I do. She was a very dear friend of mine."

"Was?"

"Yes. You didn't hear?" My heart raced as I realized Chastity had no idea.

"Hear what?"

"Ceazia passed." I looked down as my eyes began to fill with tears.

"Damn, I had no idea." Chastity paused as she stared into space. "Well, our work here is done." She stood up. "You're hired. Welcome to the team. I have to tell you, I don't normally hire on the spot. Most girls who apply have to come in during the week on amateur nights until they prove they're ready for a scheduled set. But on the strength of *C*, you've got the job. When would you like to start?"

"Tonight!" I said, full of excitement.

"See you then."

"Thank you!" I walked out of the office. "And thank you," I said as I looked up to the sky. "I knew you were looking down on me. I love you, girl." I sent love up to Ceazia.

Chapter 8

"Sex with You Is Like . . ."

Calico

I don't know if it was the six-hour plane ride from Los Angeles to Norfolk, or if it was the weed that I had been smoking on my way to Jewel's house, because I was so high, I drove past her house three times before I realized it. But whatever was the cause, all I knew was, I was horny as a muthafucka, and I wanted some pussy.

"So you like my place?" Jewel asked me as we walked into her immaculate home.

I had to give it up to her because, from a quick look at things, her spot impressed me. And I wasn't the easiest person to impress. "Yeah, I'm actually feeling it." I smiled.

Jewel pointed out all the details and showed off at the same time. "I bought it brand-new about a year ago. So when they were building it, I had the builder put in all custom shit—Canadian maple floors, granite countertops, stainless steel kitchen appliances, all of that."

I nodded my head, but I didn't verbally respond to Jewel. I walked behind her and followed her from the living room to the kitchen and then back toward the living room.

Jewel had on an Ed Hardy wife-beater, and I could tell that she didn't have a bra on, because her firm, full titties were packed so tight into her shirt that I could see the full imprint of her nipples. She also had on some black Twisted Heart sweatpants and a pair of Gucci slippers. I couldn't keep my eyes off of Jewel's sexy feet, and as horny as I was at that moment, it didn't take much for me to get turned on.

As I walked behind her and watched her fat ass jiggling around in her sweatpants, my dick instantly got hard. "You ain't wearing no panties, are you?" I knew that my question had caught Jewel off guard, but I could tell that she didn't take offense.

She turned around and said with a smile, "Excuse you."

"You and your sexy-ass feet." I grabbed my crotch.

"Calico, stop playing. Let me finish showing you the rest of the house. Come on, let's go upstairs," Jewel instructed me as she reached the base of the semi-spiral staircase that led to the second floor.

"But am I right, though?" I asked.

"Calico, please."

"You owe me one."

"What you mean?" Jewel asked.

"One sexual pleasure," I said, reminding her of the bet she'd lost.

"Fuck!" Jewel yelled then turned toward me and smiled as she slowly pulled down on the front of her sweatpants, exposing her Brazilian waxed pussy to me. And just as quickly as she had flashed me, she pulled her pants back up. "Satisfied?" she asked, and she started to head up the steps.

"Oh shit! That's what I'm talking about!" I said as I caught up to her and wrapped my arms around her from behind.

I started to caress both of Jewel's breasts and kissed on

her neck. Jewel made a slight erotic gasp. I could tell that she was enjoying how I kissed and touched her body.

"Baby, you giving me chills," she said. "We can't do this now. Come on, stop. Let's chill." She removed my hands from her breast.

"I want chu right now," I whispered into her ear, kissing on it at the same time. And without her permission, I slid my right hand into her pants and started massaging her clit with my middle finger.

"Oh my God!" Jewel said.

I could tell that she was turned on, because of how wet her pussy was. I slipped my middle finger into her pussy and I started to finger-fuck her right there on the steps.

Jewel began moving her hips as if she was dancing to a reggae song and she was getting more and more turned on by the minute. "We gotta stop, baby," she said to me, while trying to remove my hand from her pants.

But I could tell that she wasn't really putting up any true resistance. She turned and faced me, and when she did, she dropped her cell phone on the steps.

I turned her back around so that her back was again to my chest, and I pulled her sweatpants down to her ankles.

"Calico, okay, wait, just let me get my phone," she said to me.

My dick harder than Chinese arithmetic, I could care less about her phone. "Fuck the phone." I stepped on it with my foot and slid it down to the next step below the one I was standing on.

While I palmed Jewel's ass cheeks with my left hand, I used my right hand to quickly unbuckle my LRG jeans. I was feeling like a dog in heat, so I didn't bother to take off my shoes, my jewelry, my shirt, or anything. I simply pulled my pants and my boxers down around my thighs so that my dick was fully exposed.

At this point, Jewel had slipped out of her slippers and had managed to fully work herself out of her sweatpants. I bent her over and slid my dick into her pussy from the back and started pumping like a porno star.

Jewel reached her hands forward and balanced herself by placing her right hand on the steps in front of her and her left hand onto the handrail next to her.

"Aaaahhhh fuck!" Jewel screamed out. "Calico, your dick feels so damn good!"

"Your pussy is tight as hell! I wanted to fuck you from the first day I saw you!" I steadily continued to fuck her.

I pulled her wife-beater forward so that her titties were fully exposed. I watched them sway back and forth as I hit her ass doggy-style. The sight alone of her big ass slamming against my stomach was enough to make me cum, but I knew that I couldn't cum before her. And from the way she was throwing her ass back at me, I could tell that she was really close to reaching her peak.

Jewel turned her head and said to me, "Baby, we ain't even using a condom."

"I know, I know. Don't worry, though. I'll make sure I pull out before I cum," I said, hoping that would be enough to persuade Jewel to let me finish fucking her.

Jewel didn't respond, so I took that as my cue to keep going. I grabbed a fistful of her hair and pulled on it, and fucked her even harder.

"Oh, yes! I love that! Fuck me harder!" she screamed.

I complied with her instructions, and about thirty seconds later she let me know that she was cumming. And not long after that, I could feel myself about to cum as well. Her pussy felt so damn good, I didn't want to pull out, but I had given her my word that I would.

"Turn around," I instructed Jewel as I pulled my dick out of her pussy. "I wanna cum on your titties!"

She turned around and sat on one of the steps and cupped her titties so that she was pressing them together. I stroked my dick a few times and then shot cum all over her breasts.

"Oh shit! That was good! I needed that!" I said to her.

Jewel looked at me and smiled. And then she stood up and mushed me in my face. "Nigga, you better have a got-damn condom next time!"

"Definitely," I said.

I pulled up my pants and I began to fix my belt buckle. I watched Jewel use her wife-beater to wipe the cum off her breasts. I was satisfied that I had accomplished my mission.

My mission was to get her to totally trust me so that she would be willing to do anything for me that I needed her to do. I had already pacified her with a little a bit of bread, and seeing that she had let me so easily fuck her "raw dawg" with no condom, I knew she had to trust a nigga. But, then again, at the same time I had to be smart, because Jewel could've just as easily been a hoe-ass trick who was just trying to set me up to snake me somehow.

Chapter 9

"All Chicks Are the Same"

Touch

"Jewel! What up, ace?" I answered my cell phone, happy to hear from my homie. "Hello?" I said, after not hearing any response on the other end. I held my phone forward to double-check the name that was on the screen, and it was definitely Jewel's name that appeared on my phone.

My first thought was that we had a bad cell phone connection, and I was about to hang up and call her right back. But then I heard some noise in the background. I listened more closely to try and decipher what it was that I was hearing. After listening closely, I realized that Jewel must have called my cell phone by mistake.

"Aaahhh fuck! Calico, your dick feels so damn good."

"What the fuck?" I said out loud. I balled my face up.

"Your pussy is tight as hell. I wanted to fuck you from the first day I saw you."

I couldn't believe what I was hearing. I was hoping it was just some kind of sick trick that Jewel and Calico were playing on me.

"Baby, we ain't even using a condom."

"I know, I know. Don't worry, though. I'll make sure I pull out before I cum."

"Oh, yes! I love that! Fuck me harder!"

As I continued to listen, I could literally hear the sound of skin slapping against skin, so I knew that Jewel and Calico were actually fucking. I twisted my lips and shook my head in disgust. *How the fuck Jewel gone sell out like that?* I couldn't believe this shit I was hearing.

"Turn around. I wanna cum on your titties."

"Oh shit! That was good! I needed that."

"Nigga, you better have a gotdamn condom next time!"

"Definitely."

I listened for a little while longer and I could hear Jewel and Calico rummaging around and making small talk with each other. It sounded like they were done fucking. Fuming, I hung up on my end. I didn't know what pissed me off more, the fact that Jewel was acting like a naïve schoolgirl and was actually falling into Calico's trap, or that Calico would disrespect the game and fuck with Jewel on that level.

I tried to go back to watching sports highlights on ESPN, but I had to admit, hearing that phone call had fucked my head up. Jewel was my female road dawg, and although we had never really caught feelings for one another, there was a small part of me that kind of made me feel like she was my girl. So listening to that phone call and hearing Calico fuck her was kind of like me hearing some nigga fuck my bitch. I could just picture that shit. I ain't gon' lie, a nigga was real fucked-up.

I got up and went to my kitchen to get a Heineken. After I cracked it open and took a few swigs, I decided to call Jewel. I dialed her number, and her cell phone just rang out to voice mail. I waited a few minutes and called her house phone, and again she didn't pick up, and it rang out to voice mail.

Yo, I can't believe she fucking falling for that clown-ass nigga, I said to myself as I walked back to my flat-screen television.

What was wild was, as I sat and watched ESPN, the announcers started talking about that old beef that Kobe Bryant and Shaquille O'Neal had a few years ago when they were on the same team. Stuart Scott from ESPN, the cool black dude that all of the other announcers try to be like, kept it real, saying how it was wrong for Kobe to snitch on Shaquille O'Neal like he'd done when he got caught cheating on his wife. He continued on and was saying how in his mind that was probably the last straw for Shaquille O'Neal and that was probably what made him demand a trade to the Miami Heat.

Then he summed it up by saying that at the end of the day it also was probably just a situation where Kobe's ego and Shaquille's ego were just too fucking big for the two of them to be on the same team together.

It was crazy for me to be hearing the commentators talking about that because, in a lot of ways, that was how I was feeling about me and Calico. Here that nigga was from Cali-muthafuckin'-fornia, and he was all the way on the East Coast, in my town, coming across like he owned the muthafucking key to the city, and like he was the man and shit. Granted, Calico was a big reason why a lot of niggas was eating, and he and I had done a lot of business together, but that nigga had crossed the line this time.

At one point this nigga used to be humble and about his bread. Fast-forward a year or two, and the nigga is all Hollywood all of a sudden. Now the nigga wants to fuck every bitch, floss in all the clubs, and do all kinds of high-profile shit. I'd learned a long time ago, whenever a nigga stops being humble and it starts becoming all about them, that's when it's time to cut niggas off and stop fucking with them. I mean, I seen it time and time again—Niggas go and get Hollywood, and then they get fucking sloppy and fuck shit up for everybody. Hell, that's how I ended up in the penitentiary.

Calico was my man, so I knew exactly what he was trying to do. He was planning on using Jewel's ass so that he could use her crib as a stash house, like he was doing with a bunch of other chicks. He was gonna chill in her spot for a spell and run his product from there, cook up, stash some money and a few guns. Then when he felt like her spot was getting hot, he would be on to the next chick.

Fuck that nigga Calico! I thought to myself. *This is my motherfucking town!* I was gonna play shit cool, but it was definitely time for me to start making moves so that I could phase Calico out. I had a plan, but to be honest, the easiest plan would have been to pay one of those young-ass cats trying to make a name for themselves to make his ass disappear. It wasn't like he was untouchable. And, after all, my name was *Touch*.

Chapter 10

"Love & Hate"

Jewel

Sexy muthafucka. I looked at a sleeping Calico. My body ached from a night of continuous fucking as I rose from the bed and headed toward the bathroom. I looked at my reflection in the mirror with shame. I spoke to my reflection. "You are officially a bona fide whore!" I couldn't believe the shit I'd done. Not only did I let this nigga fuck me as soon as he got there, but I let him fuck me raw! I guess when a bitch is on a one-month drought, the pussy has a mind of its own. I ain't gon' front—I wanted some dick, but a bitch should have at least had a little class about herself. All I can say was, at least that shit was good. I knew it had to be something golden about this nigga for him to have so many bitches, yet no drama. Shit, the money and dick alone was enough to keep my mouth shut! Plus, this nigga's body was as flawless as a coin in mint condition.

I jumped in the shower and threw on some clothes so that I'd look my best when Calico woke.

The time was nine o'clock. Remembering Touch needed me to take him to the airport, I called him up.

He answered the phone with little emotion, "What's up?"

"Ugh! What's wrong with you?" I said, noticing he wasn't himself.

"Nothing. What's the deal?" Touch responded with the same tone as before.

"Well, I just remember you said something about the airport the other day. When you going?"

"Today."

"Today? Why didn't you call me?"

"I was gonna just use short-term parking."

"No, I'm taking you. What time is your flight?"

"Three o'clock."

"Okay. Meet me at my house, and we'll leave from here."

"A'ight."

"Cool," I responded then hung up the phone.

Realizing I only had a few hours before it was time to take Touch to the airport, I rushed to cook Calico breakfast. Thinking of something quick, I decided to cook omelets.

Before I was finished, Calico was on his way into the kitchen. "Yeah, I better have some breakfast waiting. Especially when you be cooking that nigga Touch breakfast." He hugged me from behind.

"Whatever, nigga. Don't think you gon' be getting this kind of treatment every morning, though." I let him know the deal right off the bat.

"I ain't trying to hear that shit. You gon' do whatever it takes to keep a nigga happy," Calico said confidently.

Yep. As long as you keeping this bitch happy by keeping the money coming, I thought.

"What you smirking at?" Calico asked.

I guess my thoughts were written all over my face. "Nothing. Just thinking about what you said."

"So you ain't trying to keep a nigga happy?"

I responded with a question just as important, "You trying to keep a bitch happy?"

"No doubt. I got you. I thought you already knew that."

"Nah. That could just be preliminary game you throwing. You can see from how I do things that I'm not your average chick. I like nice things and love having my way. So are you really trying to hold me down?" I asked, to see where his head was really at.

"Jewel, I got you, baby. Relax. Let shit take its course." Calico took a seat at the breakfast bar.

"Okay then. Well, I got you," I said, as I handed him his food.

I cleaned up the kitchen and straightened the small mess we'd made in my bedroom as Calico ate.

When he finished he met me in the bedroom. "I'm about to run out," he said. "You didn't tell anybody I was here, did you?"

"Nope," I said, just now remembering he'd told me not to tell anyone of his visit. Luckily, I hadn't told anyone.

"You sure about that? Not even your homeboy?"

"I guess you're referring to Touch but, to answer your question, no, I didn't tell him."

"Cool. Well, I'm going on a few runs. I'll hit you up when I'm done."

"Okay."

Deep inside, I wanted to put up an argument, because this trip was supposed to be all about me, but I knew that I had to take Touch to the airport and I'd told him to meet him at my house. So I kinda needed Calico to leave so that I didn't blow his cover. I kissed him on the lips before he headed out the door.

"Damn, I've got another winner!" I said to myself as I watched Calico jump in his rental car from my bedroom window.

Just then my phone rang, interrupting my thoughts. "Hey, Boobie," I answered, realizing it was Sasha.

"Hey, baby. I've been dancing at the club, and it's turning out great! I'm really making some money!"

"That's good. I'm so happy for you. I'm making me a little change myself." I quickly began to share the news of Calico with Sasha.

"Huh? What you doing? I know your ass ain't on no pole!"

"Hell nah, girl. I finally got this nigga Calico where I want him."

"Who?"

"Calico. Touch friend. The one from the bar that night, remember?" I tried refreshing Sasha's memory.

"Oh, okay. Damn, how you do that?"

"Well, you know he took me shopping on our first date. That was an indication of how he breaks bread. But, anyway, I talked him into coming to VA, and this nigga sent me three grand, Western Union, before he even got here," I bragged.

"And what did you have to do to get that three grand?" Sasha asked, sounding all sarcastic and shit.

"What chu mean?"

"I know you gave up some ass."

"To be honest, yeah, I did, but that was *after* I'd received three stacks and a shopping spree, enough to ensure there was more to come. And if not, it still covered the expense," I spat back, letting her know I knew what I was doing.

"Umph . . . well, good for you, I guess. I got three stacks too, but it took me a few days in the strip club to gain that."

"Well, why you not there looking for a nigga? I gave you the rules. Shit, utilize those muthafuckas!"

"I hear you."

Just then I heard a horn blow in front of my house. Touch was out front.

"Well, let me go. I have to take Touch to the airport. He's

coming down your way, as a matter of fact. You gon' be at the club tonight?"

"Do I have a choice?"

"What's that suppose to mean?" I asked, hoping she would elaborate. I'd had just about enough of Sasha's sour-ass attitude. I really hoped it wasn't envy I smelt in the air. Sasha and I had the same opportunities in life. She just chose an alternate route. Was I to blame?

"I ain't got it like you. I got to struggle to get mine."

"Well, I'm trying to help a sister out. I'm gon' send Touch up there to show some support."

"Thanks . . . I guess."

"Yep," I said, totally ignoring her stupid-ass attitude. *Bitch!* I thought to myself before ending our phone call.

I headed out the door to meet Touch. "What's up, big homie?" I pressed the unlock button to my truck.

"Ain't shit." Touch climbed into the truck.

I tried to figure out what was up with my buddy. "Damn, you still down, nigga? What the fuck? Guess you got baby momma blues and too ashamed to tell me or something."

"Nah, it ain't my baby momma this time. Someone else is fucking up. Looks like that shit is contagious," Touch said, confusing the hell out of me.

I could tell from the way Touch was talking, he was very disappointed in someone, and it didn't look like he was try-ing to talk about it, so I chose to leave it alone.

"Well, you know Sasha is in Atlanta now," I said, chang-ing the subject.

"Oh yeah?"

"Yep. She's working at this club called Bottoms Up. You and some of your boys should go check her, show her some support."

"I'm-a make sure I do that," Touch said, showing interest in something for the first time since we'd been together.

Fifteen minutes later, we were at Norfolk International Airport. I pulled up to the Delta departure terminal. "Here's your stop."

"Thanks." Touch pulled out his wallet, pulled out a fifty, and handed it to me.

"Have a safe trip." I grabbed the money with one hand and leaned forward to hug him with the other.

"Nah. You be safe. You're gonna need it more than me." Touch jumped out the truck without hugging me.

I sat in awe for about thirty seconds, trying to register what the fuck had just happened. When I finally came to my senses, I looked up to see him walking through the automatic doors and into the airport. The nigga never even looked back.

He's on that Gemini split-personality bullshit for real, I thought to myself before peeling off.

Chapter 11

"Down-ass Chick"

Calico

By the time I got back to Jewel's house, it was close to seven o'clock, and I knew that I hadn't kept my word.

"You know you done lost a whole lotta points with me, right?" Jewel said to me as soon as I walked into her crib. She didn't even give me a chance to respond and kept going in on me. "I thought this little trip you took out here was supposed to be all about me! I sure as hell can't tell, from the way you running the streets. Can *I* get some attention, gotdamit?"

I couldn't help but look at Jewel and smile. I loved her sassy-ass attitude and her whole style.

"What the fuck are you smiling about? I don't see shit funny!"

I didn't answer Jewel. I just walked up to her and smacked her on her ass and continued on my way to her kitchen to get myself something to drink.

"Mr. Burroughs, don't fuck with me! You said this trip was supposed to be about me, and that no one was going to even know you were here. But, from the looks of it, this trip seems like it's all about you. You already got some pussy, I cooked and fed your ass, and then you have the audacity to spend the entire day on the street. What the fuck?"

"Jewel, I told you that I got you."

"Yeah, whatever, nigga. I can't tell. You just seem a little too damn comfortable."

After Jewel said that, I sipped on some fruit punch that I had just poured for myself and put the glass on her granite countertop. I walked out the front door toward my rental car.

"Where are you going now?" she asked with a major attitude.

I didn't say anything as I pressed the button on the keychain to release the trunk. I reached inside and took out a shopping bag, and headed back into the house. "This is for you. I hope you like it," I said as I handed Jewel the shopping bag and walked into the living room and turned on the flat-screen.

"Ahhhhhhhhhh!"

When I heard Jewel screaming, I knew she loved the gift.

"Calico! I can't believe you!" Jewel came running and jumped into my arms.

"Oh, now I'm Calico again? A minute ago, I was Mr. Burroughs."

"Yeah, but a minute ago you hadn't given me a green crocodile Hermes bag."

I couldn't help but chuckle at Jewel as she loosened herself from me and proceeded to parade around the living room, showing off her bag as if she was a runway supermodel.

"The girls are gonna be so sick when they see me rocking this bag."

"Yep! And they'll have nine thousand reasons to be sick,"

I said, alluding to how much I'd paid for the bag. "Now, do you believe me when I say I got you?"

"Yes, sirrr," Jewel playfully responded.

Jewel's mood had instantly switched up from pissed-off and agitated to warm and cheery. That was a sure indication of how to deal with her in the future.

"Come here and let me give you kisses," Jewel said to me as she walked toward me, her lips puckered up for a kiss.

I kissed her soft lips and felt on her ass, and two seconds later she was back admiring her bag in the mirror.

"So, listen, here's the deal. That bag is my down payment on a shopping spree. Tomorrow, we'll go shopping, but tonight let's just go out to eat and then hit the strip club or something," I said.

"Okay. But I thought you didn't want nobody to know you were in town? You sure you wanna go to the strip club?"

"Yeah. Actually, there's a whole lot of shit on my mind right now, and the strip club has always been the best way for me to unwind and get my head right."

"Ocean Cabaret? Hell, nah. That's not a real strip club. It's too fucking bourgeoisie for my taste. Let's hit up Purple Rain," I explained to Jewel as we headed out of McCormick & Schmick's Seafood Restaurant.

"Oh, so you like that ghetto shit then. Okay, Purple Rain is cool with me. I can check my girl Shakira. But, for the record, there you go with shit being about you again. Remember, your trip to Virginia was supposed to be about me."

I looked at Jewel and nodded my head as we pulled off in her white Range Rover. Jewel had forgotten her iPod, so she was forced to listen to the radio. When she turned on the radio, one of my favorite Jay-Z songs were on, "Can I Get a 'Fuck You.'"

"Oh, turn that shit up!" I yelled. I began reciting the lyrics along with Jay-Z. I reached over and turned the volume down, and then I asked Jewel, "So if I wasn't a nigga with figgas, would you come around me or would you clown me?"

Jewel just looked at me and smiled, and then she turned the volume back up. Right on cue, she began to recite the female lyrics of the song. She reached and turned the volume back down, and the two of us started laughing at each other.

"Wait, hold up. Don't you ever touch a black man's radio! What's wrong witchu?" I asked, trying to imitate Chris Tucker in *Rush Hour*. I turned the radio back up and started to recite the chorus to the song, doing the wop dance at the same time.

Now can you bounce for me, bounce for me,
Can ya, can ya bounce wit' me, bounce wit' me . . .

"Oh my God, Calico, you are so crazy!" Jewel laughed at me.

Not much longer after that, we arrived at the strip club. The shit was extra packed. There was some porn star chick named Pinky, who was making a guest appearance that night, so that was the reason for the large crowd.

As soon as I walked in the spot, it was like a freaking love fest. Dancer after dancer kept coming up to me saying hello, as did some of the fellas that I knew from the streets.

Jewel said to me, "I see you a little ghetto celebrity in here."

One of the dancers asked me, "Yo, Calico, you gon' make it rain tonight?"

"Nah, baby, not tonight. I'm just chillin."

When Jewel and I sat down, I ordered a bottle of Hennessy for myself, and a bottle of Nutcracker for her. As soon

as our drinks arrived, Jewel started in with the questions.
"Okay, so tell me, what got your head so fucked-up that you
needed to come in here and get it right?"

I drank a glass of Hennessy and then I exhaled some air
from my lungs. "It's just that I'm real hot right now," I
screamed into Jewel's ear over the loud music. "It's a lot of
jealous-ass snitch muthafuckas out here that wanna see me
fall, you know?"

Jewel drank some of her Nutcracker. "You'll be okay,
pookie face," she said.

I shook my head. I didn't totally let Jewel in on everything that I knew, but the fact was, I had just recently found
out that I had been secretly indicted by the Virginia Commonwealth Attorney. And, from what I was hearing from my
man who was fucking one of the female assistant Commonwealth attorneys, Touch had snaked my ass, and it was his
testimony to the grand jury that really led to my indictment.
I hated to believe that my man for so long would do some
shit like that, but you could never really trust a nigga, when
it comes to the drug game.

I knew that I was taking a big chance being in Virginia,
with all this going on, and an even bigger chance being out
at the strip club. But the thing was, deep inside, I knew that
Touch had snaked me. I never wanted to show him the cards
I was holding, so I purposely played things cool with him,
hung out with him, and did everything as normal.

Truth be told, one of the main reasons that I had come to
visit Jewel was so that I could collect on the hundred and
fifty thousand that Touch had owed me, and to set him up
to have him killed. I mean, I wasn't no dummy. I knew that
a dead Touch couldn't pay me the bread that he owed me, so
I had to get my dough first, and then hit his ass.

My plan was to butter up Jewel with gifts and all, just like
I was doing, so that she'd be distracted. I needed her dis-

tracted because I didn't want her suspecting anything that was about to go down with me and Touch. This way, when Touch did get blasted, she would never suspect that I had anything to do with it. I knew I had to move cautiously.

Although Touch was a pretty chill dude, he did have a dark side that would surprise any unsuspecting nigga. Shit, that's one of the reasons I had originally partnered up with him. And that's why I'd conveniently sent Diana his way. So that I could keep tabs on him, and she could distract him when necessary. I knew if I threw her a few dollars I could rely on her to hold things down. Plus, I even had his no-good baby mother on the team. Although she had no idea, she was probably gonna end up causing his death.

With Touch on my mind, I pulled out my cell phone and placed a call to him. "What's good, baby boy?" I said when Touched answered the phone. I then excused myself from the lounge table that I was sitting at and made my way to the bathroom, where it was quieter and I could hear better.

"Everything's good. What's the deal?"

"You got that for me?" I said, referring to the hundred and fifty thousand.

"Yeah, yeah, no doubt."

"So where you at?" I asked.

Touch explained to me that he was down in Atlanta and that he would be back next week.

"Next fucking week? Touch, what the fuck is up? Your dough is straight or what? Keep it real with me. Last week you told me this week, and now you telling me next week? I ain't never had no issues over getting my bread from you—"

Touch cut me off. "Exactly, we ain't never had no problem, so no need to stress me. I got your dough. I'm just outta town. When I touch down, I'll get the shit to you, a'ight?"

"Whatever, man. Just hit me as soon as you touch down,

and I'll head out there the next day," I said, not wanting him to know my whereabouts.

I made it back to where Jewel was sitting. I saw her chatting with one of the dancers that went by the name Paradise. Before I could blink, Jewel winked her eye at me and told me that she was going off to get a private dance.

"Oh, okay, do you, ma."

I sat and drank glass after glass of Hennessy, and within an hour I was fucked-up. Jewel was also twisted. And after being around so much tits and ass, we were both horny as shit.

"You ready?" I asked her.

Jewel said that she was, and without making my usual rounds to tell people that I was bouncing, she and I just got up and departed from the club. I quickly peeped out the parking lot as we made our way to Jewel's Range Rover. As we pulled off and headed back toward Jewel's crib, I noticed Diana's trick-ass hollering at a couple of dudes with New York plates.

We were no more than five blocks away from the club when Jewel said, "Something's up."

"What are you talking about?"

"The fucking police are following us."

"Get the fuck outta here."

"Yeah, it's a marked car. He been following us since we left the club."

"Muthafucka! And I'm dirty too! Shit, what the fuck was I thinking?" I started to stress out.

"You dirty how?"

"I got these fucking *X* pills on me," I explained to Jewel as I pulled out the bag of ecstasy pills to show her just what the hell I was talking about.

Just at that point the cops signaled for us to pull over.

My heart was pounding.

"Give me that shit," Jewel said to me as she kept driving, disobeying the cops flashing lights.

"What?"

"Calico, give me the damn pills!"

I didn't know what Jewel was planning on doing, but I didn't want her to get bagged on no drug charge.

"Nah, Jewel, I got this."

She reached over and grabbed the clear bag of X pills. She began unbuckling her tight-ass jeans with one hand, and steered the car with her other hand. "I'm putting this shit in my pussy. We'll be good."

Jewel was like a magician, the way she squirmed out of her tight jeans just enough to expose her pussy and stuff the bag of drugs inside.

I said to her as she pulled over, "My name is Martin Green, if they ask you."

She looked at me. "Okay."

Before we could blink, there was one cop on the driver's side window, and another on the passenger side. They were both shining their lights inside the car after Jewel and I had rolled down our windows.

The cop asked Jewel, "Miss, can you tell me why it took you three extra blocks of driving before you pulled over?"

"I pulled over as soon as I saw your lights in my rearview mirror, officer."

The cop shook his head and asked for Jewel's license and registration and insurance. "Is this your car?" he asked.

"Yes."

"Okay, the reason I'm pulling you over is because of your tint," he explained. "You can't have your tint so dark. It's illegal."

Jewel responded, "I didn't know that, officer."

"Okay, sit tight. I'll be back."

As soon as the cop walked off, Jewel exhaled. " I am drunk as a skunk. I hope he can't smell that shit."

"Nah, you good. Just relax."

"Damn, that was quick," Jewel said in reference to how quick the cop had returned to our car.

"Ms. Diaz, can you step out of the car, please?"

I yelled over to the cop on the driver's side, "For what?"

"Sir, just put your hands on the dashboard and relax," the cop on my side said to me.

The cop said to Jewel, "Turn around and face the car," and he whipped out his handcuffs and placed her under arrest.

"This is crazy! What are you arresting me for? Tinted windows?"

"No, ma'am. Your license is suspended. That's what I'm arresting you for." The officer frisked Jewel.

The cop on my side asked me, "You have a driver's license?"

I shook my head no, and at that point, my mouth became dry as shit.

Jewel spoke up and told the cop who'd handcuffed her that it would be all right for me to drive her car home.

"Not without a driver's license," the cop explained.

"Do you have any identification on you?" the cop asked me.

"No."

"Do you have a name? Date of birth?"

"Martin Green. 7/22/78."

The cop walked Jewel to the back of the police car, while the other cop radioed in the information that I'd just given him.

For five minutes I sat in limbo in Jewel's Range Rover. Then the other cop that had walked Jewel to the squad car came back over to the Range Rover and whispered something into the other cop's ear.

"Can you step out of the car please?"

I obeyed, not fully knowing what was up.

"Michael Burroughs, you have the right to remain silent. Anything you say can and will be used against you . . ."

Muthafucka! I shook my head and clenched my teeth in anger, wondering just how the fuck was I gonna get myself out of this sling that I'd suddenly found myself in.

Chapter 12

"Payback's a Bitch"

Touch

After I hung up the phone, I shouted, "Bitch-ass nigga!" Calico was really becoming a pain in my ass.

I immediately called Jewel, and her phone rang out to voice mail. "Jewel, what's up? This is Touch. Call me back as soon as you get this message. Gone."

I made my way into Bottoms Up. I needed a drink in the worst way. I headed to the bar and ordered a double shot of Grey Goose and took it straight to the head.

"Oh shit! Hey, Touch. What's good, homie? Is this like a fucking high-school reunion or some shit?"

I squinted my eyes, trying to figure out who the fuck it was that was talking to me.

"It's me, man. Diablo."

"Oh what's the deal, Diablo?" I extended my hand to Diablo and gave him a pound.

The deejay shouted into the microphone, "Coming to the stage, we got Juicy on stage one, and Malibu on stage two. Show them some love, fellas."

Diablo said to me, "That thick shit right over there on the stage, Malibu, that's what's up."

I looked over to the stage and saw Sasha wiping down the pole on the stage, preparing to do her thing. I have to admit, looking at Sasha instantly made my dick rise.

I hadn't seen Diablo in years. I'd heard that he'd moved to Atlanta from Virginia and was doing his thing and getting money down there. But I never really liked the dude. I always tolerated his ass, but I never really fucked with him like that. He wasn't an enemy per se, but he wasn't a real nigga. He was one of those niggas that always managed to get over and shit. Besides, that nigga ain't like me back in high school because he thought I was knocking Jewel off when they were kicking it.

Diablo ordered a bottle of Rosé, and we popped the bottle and drank champagne, and kicked it.

Just before Sasha was finished with her routine, I walked up to the stage and threw three hundred-dollar bills at her.

"Oh shit! Thank you," Sasha said, looking at the money only and not even realizing it was me.

I screamed out to her, "Sasha, what up, girl?"

"Oh my God! Touch! What's up, baby? I didn't even realize that was you. Wait right there. I'll be there in a minute," Sasha said as she walked around the stage, butt-ass naked in her stilettos, picking up the money that she'd just made and tossing it in a tall, clear garbage bag.

I turned around to see Diablo hawking my ass like a fucking stalker.

"So, Diablo, where you gonna be? Let me get your number so I can kick it witchu before I bounce back to VA."

Diablo gave me his number. "So you down here buying them thangs?"

I knew he was referring to weight, but that wasn't the

reason I had come to Atlanta. "Nah, I'm actually down here looking at some real estate that I'm trying to buy."

"Oh, okay. That's what's up. So, if you need them thangs, holler at your boy." Diablo gave me a pound and walked off.

Just as Diablo walked off, Sasha came up to me and gave me a kiss on my cheek.

"Sasha, I forgot you had all that damn booty up under them clothes," I said, still admiring her body. "You make a nigga wanna wife your ass."

"Nigga, please. Everybody wanna wife a bitch when she butt-ass naked," Sasha said jokingly.

"So what's up?"

"Nothing. I'm just up in here working, trying to get my swagger back. I been going through it lately."

I couldn't help but to continue to stare at her body.

"Touch, if you don't stop . . ."

"Yo, come on, I want a private dance. You working, right?" I grabbed her by the hand, and we walked downstairs toward the VIP rooms. "It's twenty dollars a song, right?"

"Yep." Sasha smiled at me and took the lead, walking in front of me toward a leather couch in the VIP room.

I handed her one hundred dollars. She sat me down and asked me if it was all right if she took off her shoes. I nodded yes, and she took off her shoes and waited for the next song to come on. When it did, she started dancing for me.

I asked her, "You know I always had a crush on you?"

"Yeah, whatever. You know you coulda had me whenever you wanted me, but your nose was always up Jewel's ass."

Sasha sat her soft, plump ass on my lap and started grinding on my rock-hard dick.

"So I *coulda* had you?" I asked. "So you saying I can't have you *now*?"

Sasha turned around and faced me in a straddled position. Then she leaned in and started kissing me on my neck and ear. As she kissed me on my ear, she whispered, "You know good and well that Jewel would have a fit if I was fucking witchu."

At that point Sasha had turned me on to the point where I was ready to stick my dick in her pussy right there and fuck her on the spot. Jewel and her feelings was the last thing on my mind right then. Besides, she was banging Calico. Maybe she needed a taste of her own medicine.

"We both grown," I said. "What we do is between me and you. Jewel ain't got to know what we do."

Sasha didn't respond. She just kept grinding on me and doing her thing. Then she reached her hand in my pants and started stroking my dick. "Ummmhhh," she moaned in my ear, "I didn't know you were working with all this."

"So now you know." I wanted to just stand up and bend her ass over and fuck her.

The last song of my five songs had just started playing, and I said to Sasha, "I know everything I say to you, you gon' go back and tell Jewel what I said. But ya girl's been on some bullshit lately, on the real."

"Oh my God! Who you telling?" Sasha shot back at me. "I thought it was just me, but I did notice she was acting funny and shit. It's like sometimes she can be there and care for me and look out for me, but it's like I don't know if it's always genuine 'cause, in the next breath, she's always flaunting shit and trying to down my ass and show off and shit."

I nodded my head, and then we both stood up because my time was up.

"So, listen," I whispered into her ear, "I'm staying at the Ritz Carlton in Buckhead across from Lenox. Why don't you come chill wit' me when you get up outta here?"

Sasha nodded her head. "Okay, but I probably wouldn't be leaving until around three in the morning."

"It's all good. I still be here."

She kissed me on the cheek then walked off.

I watched her every move as her sexy ass walked in her stilettos and the white slingshot bikini that she was wearing. I couldn't wait to get her to my room so I could smash that ass.

Chapter 13

"In the Heat of the Night"

Sasha

Although I was dancing for a nigga and he was making it rain, my mind was on other things. I watched the clock constantly, waiting for three o'clock to hit. Hell, even two thirty. Anything just so that I could get the fuck out of dodge. All I could think of was Touch. That muthafucka literally had my pussy dripping. A bitch had to go to the dressing room and clean up with a baby wipe after lap-dancing with him. A few more songs and I could have busted right on his lap.

"Yo, shawty," the dude I danced for said with his deep down South country accent.

"Yes?" I responded full of attitude because he'd disrupted my day-dreaming about Touch.

"Make it clap or something for a nigga," he said, noticing my lack of energy.

"Okay, baby, I got you."

I figured I may as well straighten up and drain this nigga then call it a night. I danced for him and his boys for another ten songs then I was out.

I stopped by Touch's table on the way to the dressing room to let him know I was packing up. As soon as I packed my things and was ready to head out the dressing room door, the realization of what I was about to do settled in, and my heart began to race. I knew that Jewel would kill me if she found out. There was no way I could do it. I took a deep breath, grabbed my dance bag, and walked toward Touch to break the news to him.

He handed me a shot as soon as I walked up. "Drink this."

"What is it?"

"Patrón."

I took it down in one gulp. Hell, I needed that shit.

"You ready?" he asked as soon as I finished.

"Well—"

"Well, what?" Touch whispered in my ear then gently kissed me on my neck.

My knees got weak, and my head collapsed in his hand. I almost came from that alone. My neck was my weak spot, and it was as though this nigga knew it or something. I forced out the words, "Touch . . . I can't do this."

There was a slight awkward pause before he spoke up. Surprisingly, he gave in without a fight. "A'ight, cool. I don't want to force you. Just have a few drinks with me before I bounce."

"That's the least I can do," I said, knowing I'd disappointed him.

We took shot after shot, Patrón for me, Grey Goose for him.

After the third one, I was feeling nice, a little too nice as a matter of fact.

I found myself getting lap-dances. I looked at Touch as Juicy, one of the dancers, gave me a passionate lap-dance. She moved across my lap slowly and caressed my body all at the same time.

I fantasized it was Touch's hands on me as she embraced my body. The feeling was too overwhelming. My mind was made up. I wanted Touch, and I wanted him at that moment. I pushed Juicy off me and approached him. "I'm ready. Let's go now."

Touch didn't say a word. He just pulled his keys out and grabbed my hand, and we headed out the door. Once outside, we agreed that I would follow him. He headed to his car, and I headed to mine.

Minutes later, we were in front of the Ritz Carlton. I gathered my composure as we headed to his room. I gave myself a pep talk as I waited for him to open the door. *Get it together, Sasha. You can do this. It's just sex. You're grown. Do you. Shit, Jewel is doing her.*

"I need to take a shower first," I said as soon as we walked through the door.

"Do your thing." Touch turned the light on in the bathroom then flopped down on the bed.

I jumped in the shower and lathered up. I was sure Touch would be asleep when I got out. I was kind of hoping he would be. At least, then I would have an excuse not to have sex. But to my surprise, Touch was wide-awake when I walked out the bathroom.

"Damn, you are sexy!" he said, admiring my naked body.

"Wait!" I said, stopping him as he proceeded toward me. "Just let me do one thing first."

I ran into the bathroom and opened my bag. I needed a little encouragement, so I pulled out an ecstasy pill and popped it in my mouth. I waited a couple of minutes and headed back to the bed.

"What? You had to shit? Don't be getting in bed with me with shit crumbs in your ass," Touch joked.

"Boy, shut up. Ain't nobody shit."

I slid beneath the sheets with Touch. His dick was already rock-hard as I began to stroke it. I didn't know if it was the

X pill or just the freak in me, but I wanted to do all kinds of things with this nigga. I pulled the covers back and straddled him. Then I began kissing him on his neck and moved down toward his nipples. I licked his nipples and bit them gently, sending erotic chills down his spine.

Next, I moved my way toward his penis. Now that was my joy! Like a jumbo Blow Pop, I slowly licked all around his head. Then, out of nowhere, I began to rapidly deep-throat his dick. Touch's moans of satisfaction turned me on.

"You better not cum. I haven't even started with this dick yet." I stroked it with my right hand then began to suck it.

I took a pause and juggled his balls and licked that little piece of sensitive skin beneath them, causing him to quiver every now and then. Confident that I'd given him a blowjob better than the infamous Superhead herself, I strapped on a condom, using my lips only, then straddled his dick. Touch moaned as I sat my warm, fat, wet pussy on top of him.

"Look at this fat pussy," I demanded as I bounced up and down on top of him.

"Damn," Touch said as he watched my pussy grip his manhood with each movement.

I could tell the image alone made him want to bust, but not before I got mine. I fucked him like a dog in heat, until I felt myself reaching my peak.

"You want to cum, baby?" I asked him.

"Yeah," he said between moans.

"Okay. I want you to cum with me. I'm about to cum, baby. Cum with me," I yelled as I dug my nails into Touch's chest, and we busted together.

Moments later, while I was lying on the bed, trying to catch my breath, Touch's phone began to ring. I used that as my cue to get up and headed to the bathroom.

I heard him say, "Oh shit."

"What?" I rushed back into the room, thinking the condom had broke or some crazy shit.

"Jewel is calling."

"Don't answer it," I said frantically.

"You don't have to worry about that."

As soon as Touch's phone finished ringing my phone began to ring. I didn't know if it was a guilty conscience or what, but something was telling me that Jewel knew something was up.

Oh well, I thought to myself as I freshened up in the bathroom. *Sasha, what Jewel don't know won't hurt her. Now what you need to do is pop another one of those X pills and go back in that room for round two with Touch. As I'm sure Jewel would say herself, "Use sex to secure that nigga and his money!"*

With that in mind, I proudly headed back into the bedroom. Hell, I was just following the advice of a friend. Jewel gave me the tools, so I was utilizing them. Based on the rules I was given on how to trap a baller, Touch fit the description, and I was just being a good student by putting in the work.

Chapter 14

"A Real Gangstress or Not?"

Jewel

"**W**hy the fuck isn't anybody answering their got-damn phone!" I said to no one in particular as I waited for the cab driver to pull up to Norfolk City Jail. I'd been calling Touch and Sasha both since I'd been released and couldn't reach either of them.

Since this was my first offense and my charge wasn't major, the magistrate had agreed to let me go on a personal release bond. Calico, on the other hand, wasn't so lucky. I was able to find out that he didn't get a bond at all. Just like Calico had said when we first met, I didn't know what the fuck to do to get a nigga out of jail. That's one reason I needed to get with Touch, so I could find out my next move.

I was ecstatic when the cab pulled up. I walked to the cab like a woman with a broom stuck up her ass. I still had the plastic bag full of ecstasy pills in my pussy, and it was really beginning to feel uncomfortable. I gave the cab driver my home address and made myself comfortable in the back seat. I wasn't even trying to go to the car impound right then to pick my truck up. I felt disgusting. I reeked of jail-house funk. Three hours in jail had really taken a toll on me, and all I wanted to do was go home and shower.

I was relieved when I finally pulled up to my home. I paid the cabbie and rushed in the house.

I turned my shower water on so that it was hot as hell and got undressed. I shook my head as I pulled the bag of *X* pills from below. *What the fuck am I doing?* I opened the bag and poured out its contents into the toilet then urinated after-wards. "Fuck this!" I said aloud. I flushed the toilet then hopped in the shower.

I exhaled as the hot water from the shower ran across my body, rinsing away all the drama from the hours before. I reflected back to the moment I realized the cops were be-hind me. It was like second nature when I took those pills and pushed them inside me. Shit, I didn't know I had it in me. In that case Calico could eat his words about me not being a ride-or-die chick. Hell, if that wasn't a gangtress move, I don't know what is. But the fucked-up part about it is, now that I'd proven my status, I had no idea what was going to happen with Calico. I'd put in the work, but with his arrest, shit was looking dim, like there might not be a re-ward for me.

It was episodes just like this that made me remember why dope boys were never on the top of my list. Not only was their money not long enough, but shit, the lifestyle wasn't secure enough. Too much risk.

Needless to say I was tired as hell from everything that I had been through. I desperately wanted to speak to Touch, but since I couldn't get in contact with him, I figured that the smartest thing to do was to just lay my ass down in the bed and get some rest. I needed some sleep, so I could best figure out what the fuck had just happened, and what the fuck I was going to do next.

I crawled in my California king-sized bed. My green satin sheets never felt so good as I got comfortable beneath them. Within a matter of minutes, I was out cold and getting some much-needed sleep.

About two hours later, I was awakened by what sounded like someone knocking on my front door. I woke up disoriented and confused. Although I felt like I had been hibernating for two days or some shit, the clock said 2:30 P.M., so I knew that I had only been sleep for a few hours.

"What the fuck?" I barked as I stepped into my slippers and made my way downstairs to see who was banging on my door like they had lost their fucking mind.

My head was throbbing from having woken up so quickly, but that didn't stop me from venting the major attitude that I had. I didn't even bother to ask who it was at my door. Instead, I unlocked both locks and flung the door open.

"Do you have a gotdamn problem or something? Banging in my fucking door like you done lost your damn mind?"

There were two dudes standing at my door. One of them was big, black, and ugly, and reminded me a lot of the Notorious B.I.G. The other dude was short and stocky like a running back.

The short stocky dude asked, "Yo, where Calico at?"

Without responding to his question, I squinted my eyes and tried my hardest to figure out, had I ever seen either of those two dudes before.

"Ma, did I fucking stutter? I asked you where the fuck is Calico at?"

"What are you talking about?" My headache had suddenly disappeared, and my heart rate picked up.

The fat, ugly dude remarked, "She playing games."

At that point something told me to just slam the door and

lock it shut and try to get to my gun that was locked up-stairs. But when I attempted to close the door, the short, stocky dude prevented it from closing by sticking his foot in the way. Instantly I ran as fast as I could, trying to make it to my bedroom.

"Ugggh!" I screamed after having a fistful of my hair grabbed from the back, stopping me dead in my tracks, and being violently yanked to the ground. "Get the fuck off of me!" I screamed as I tried to get back up.

"Shorty, calm the fuck down!" The short dude put one of his white Nike Air Force One sneakers to my throat and ap-plied pressure. *Click-click.* Now with a gun cocked to my head, he continued talking. "I'm gonna ask you one more time—Where the fuck is Calico?"

Seeing my life flash before my eyes, I knew I had to speak up or else lose my life. This dude definitely seemed like he had the heart to pull that trigger. "Okay, okay, just don't kill me."

The dude gave in and released all of the pressure that he had been applying to my neck.

I started to blab, my heart still racing, "Calico was here, but he got locked up last night."

I knew I had broken the first and most important rule of the streets by running my mouth, but fuck that! This was the first time that I had actually had a gun put to my head. A bitch wasn't trying to die.

The big dude said, "She lying!"

"I swear to God, last night I was with Calico at the strip club, and the cops pulled us over when we were leaving and he got knocked." My chest was visibly inhaling and exhaling the air from my lungs, as if I had just run a marathon or something.

The guy holding the gun on me instructed the other dude, "Go check the spot."

As I sat on the floor scared as hell and at the mercy of the intruders, I could hear my house being ransacked.

The dude yelled from upstairs, "Ain't shit up in here!"

He was instructed to keep looking.

I tried my hardest to calm down, but I just couldn't. It felt like I was playing the role of Tommy's girlfriend, Keisha, in the movie *Belly*, when niggas ran up in her shit.

Five minutes more had passed by and then the Biggie look-alike came back into my living room. Once his fat ass caught his breath, he confirmed what he had said earlier.

"That's some bullshit! Get the fuck up!" the stocky dude ordered me.

I stood to my feet as I was instructed.

"We gon' get this shit up outta her! Fuck that!"

I stood up, and the room was silent.

"Yo, son, go turn on that stereo," he ordered his man.

After fiddling with my sound system, the fat dude finally figured it out, and I heard the sound of music coming from the surround-sound speakers.

"Take all your clothes off, shorty," the dude instructed me over the loud music.

"What?" I asked, looking like I was ready to shit in my pants.

"Take your muthafuckin' clothes off, bitch!"

I couldn't help but start sobbing because I knew what was coming next.

"You wanna take that pussy?" the short dude with the short-man complex asked his man.

"Hell fucking yeah," he replied, rubbing his palms together in excited anticipation like a man ready to dig into Thanksgiving dinner.

"What do y'all want? I already told y'all that Calico was locked up. I ain't lying. You can check the Norfolk City Jail," I pleaded, desperately hoping that I wouldn't get raped.

"Where the fuck is his stash at?" the dude asked me.

"I don't know. I don't fuck with Calico on that level," I replied, sounding aggravated.

The cocky dude nodded his head to the big dude, and without hesitation he began unbuckling his belt and loosening his pants. Before I could blink, his pants and his boxers were down to his knees. His fat-ass belly was so huge, it was actually covering up his little-ass dick that he reached for and began stroking.

The sight of that fat, disgusting belly and his ugly-ass dick and balls was enough to make me throw up. I knew that if this nigga's dick actually penetrated my pussy, I would have died right there on the spot.

I urged myself. *Think, Jewel! Think, think, think,*

"Okay, listen, I'm not sure, but I think Calico might have stashed something over here," I said as I walked toward a closet that was located near my front door. My heart was pounding and ready to come out of my chest, but I had to make it to my ADT alarm system keypad.

I reached for the doorknob of the closet door, and at the same time I placed my hand on the alarm system keypad that was located right next to the molding of the door and pressed the police button.

"Back up from the closet!"

I was so nervous that when he yelled, I practically jumped, but I knew that I had to hold the button down for at least five seconds. "I can't promise that there's something in here, I mean—"

"Move back from the closet," the dude said and pushed me away.

I was sure he hadn't realized that I had pressed the police button because he didn't say anything about that. He just opened the closet and began rummaging through it.

"I had just picked him up from the airport. If his bag ain't in there, it's gotta be around here somewhere," I said, trying my hardest to stall for time.

"Man, that bitch lying! Let me break her ass off real quick and let's get the fuck up outta here," Biggie Smalls Junior said. This dude still had his pants and boxers pulled down around his ankles. By now, his disgusting dick was rock-hard and three inches long, instead of the original two.

"Nah, just chill for a minute. That bitch said there was three kilos up in here, and we leaving with that shit."

Right after he was done saying that, my home phone began ringing. I was almost sure that it was the alarm company calling to check shit out before they sent the police. I wanted to answer the phone, but I froze in my tracks and waited for them to say something.

The phone stopped ringing, and everyone looked at each other.

"Go bring me the phone," the short guy said to his partner, who quickly retrieved the cordless handset. Then he instructed him to search through the caller ID. "That was probably that muthafucka Calico calling the crib."

I prayed it wasn't Calico. I was hoping like hell that it was Touch because he would have definitely known what was up, and who to reach out to in order to come check on me.

"Ain't this a bitch! Yo, son, that was the fucking alarm company," Biggie shouted.

Without warning, the short guy knocked me upside my head with the butt of his gun, spinning me around and sending me crashing to the floor, blood pouring out of the side of my head. I was literally seeing stars. I couldn't believe that I felt my own warm blood running down my chin.

The dude knelt down so that his mouth was right next to my earlobe. "You make sure you tell Calico that Sincere said that he's gonna stay all up in that ass!" After saying that, he kissed me on my earlobe and stuck his nasty-ass tongue in my mouth.

"Let's get the fuck up outta here, yo."

With that, they left, not even bothering to shut my front door and leaving me lying on the floor in my own blood, woozy and feeling like I was about to pass out. I couldn't believe what I'd just gone through.

Chapter 15

"Ready for War"

Touch

When I got the call from Jewel that some niggas had ran up in her crib and that she was hurt, I jumped on the next plane out of Atlanta and got my ass back to Virginia. I didn't know what was up, but I could bet that it had something to do with Calico. And if Jewel knew what was good for her, she would leave him the fuck alone.

I took a cab from the airport to her crib and jumped in my car. Then I headed straight to her girlfriend's crib and scooped her up and shot back to my crib with her.

I said to her while we drove toward my house, "Jewel, from all the years that I've known your ass, you ain't never lie to me. So why the fuck are you gonna start lying now? You telling me some niggas just ran up in your crib and pistol-whipped you, but they didn't take shit?"

"Yes, Touch. And why are you stressing me out? My head is killing me, and look at how I look. Look at my fucking face. Oh my God, I can't believe this shit!"

I paused because I wanted to make sure that I was acting

rationally. But after thinking to myself for a moment, I knew in my heart that this shit had something to do with Calico. "So when the last time you seen Calico?"

"Touch, I don't know."

"Did you fuck that nigga?"

"Touch, what are you talking about? Look, what you should be concerned with is dude with a New York accent named Sincere. *Sin*-fucking-*cere*, not Calico!"

I said sternly, "Jewel, did you fuck that nigga, yes or no?" then stared her in her face as to say, "I dare you to lie."

"No! Okay. All right? No, I didn't fuck Calico, got-damn!" Jewel yelled and turned her head and looked out the window, a definite sign of deceit.

I didn't have a short fuse, in terms of a temper, but whenever I felt like someone was trying to insult my intelligence or trying to play me for a fool, that shit would always cause me to lose it.

"Jewel, you fucked that nigga, and I heard the whole shit. You fucked up and called my phone by mistake, so don't sit here and lie to me. I'm ready to kill niggas behind your ass, go to jail for your ass. And you know I would die for your ass if some muthafuckas violated you the way them niggas did. But one thing I ain't gonna do is be blind to some Calico bullshit and start fighting that nigga's battles."

I looked over at Jewel as she sat slumped in the passenger seat. I could see the stress on her face. She had this look like she was ready to lash out with anger, but she kept her cool and didn't say a word.

"Now I'm gonna ask you again—Did this shit have anything to do with Calico?"

Jewel looked at me. She rolled her eyes and twisted her lips, and then she went on to tell me how Calico came to stay with her and that he didn't want anyone to know that he was in town, and that she had sworn to him that she wouldn't say anything to anybody. So, out of respect for him, she kept her mouth closed.

I slowly nodded my head, but I didn't say anything. Then there was this uneasy silence for a while.

"Touch, in case you ain't notice, I'm fucking grown. So, okay, yes, I fucked the nigga, but it was just one of those things that just kinda happened," Jewel said, giving me that same old bullshit line I'd heard a thousand other dumb-ass bitches say, including my baby mother. "It wasn't planned or nothing like that."

I smirked and then I reached for the radio and turned on the music, to break the tension that was clearly visible.

"Oh, so you're a whore now? Just randomly fucking niggas? The only chicks that I randomly fuck are tricks and whores."

"You know what—"

"What?" I asked, cutting her off.

"Yes, well then, if that makes me a whore, then I'm a fucking whore. Shit!"

"I told you from the jump how that nigga rolled. He fucks bitches, set up shop in their crib, and when shit gets hot, he bounce. You're just another fucking statistic."

The two of us finally reached my house, and I smoked a cigarette as we sat quiet in my car for a few moments not saying anything to each other. When I was done smoking, we exited the car and made it inside my crib.

For good reasons Jewel was scared to go back home and stay by herself, so I let her stay at my place, which I had no problem at all in doing.

"You know where everything is. Just make yourself at home. I gotta make some calls."

I went into my kitchen and started calling all my soldiers and told them that we was getting ready to go to war with some cat with a New York accent who went by the name of Sincere.

When I was finished with one of my calls, Jewel came into the kitchen and told me that her and Calico had gone to Purple Rain, and she told me about the arrest and all that went down with that.

"So you just had a real fucked-up run?"

"Touch, I'm all fucked-up right now."

All I could do was shake my head in pity. "Well, I'm just telling you this because, after I thought about everything, I realized that them dudes had to have seen us up in the strip club, and they must have asked around about who I was. That's the only thing I can think of as to how they knew there was a connection between me and Calico."

"Jewel, I'm gonna make everything better. I'm on the shit. You just gotta listen to me and trust me. I know how Calico gets down and what he does with chicks and how he uses them. So who knows who he ran his mouth to and about what?"

"How does my face look?"

"Jewel, you're fine. That knot is just a 'speed knot.' It's gonna go down. Besides, it's in your hairline. Once the swelling goes down, you'll be straight."

Regardless of what I said, Jewel couldn't pull herself away from standing in front of the mirror and staring into it.

"By you just staring in the mirror, it ain't gonna change nothing. Why don't you just go upstairs, get one of my T-Shirts, go take a shower, and then fix yourself a drink, and we'll just chill for the night. And if you need me to, I'll chill with you at your crib for a few days until we find this nigga Sincere."

Jewel nodded her head, and then she took her shoes off and headed to my bedroom. Before long, she came back into the living room with my New York Giants Plaxico Burress jersey in her hands and asked if it was okay to wear that.

I gave her a look as if to say, "Why are you even asking me such a stupid question?"

Jewel immediately got my drift. Before she walked off, she said, "And just for the record, I wanna be clear that I ain't nobody's trick or nobody's ho."

I knew damn well that she wasn't a whore. And, truth be told, I loved the fuck outta Jewel, like a dude loves his wife. In my mind she was like a wife to me, and it was time that I started making that shit known.

"I apologize for saying that. Jewel, you just . . ." I paused as I gathered my thoughts. "It's like you just different than most women, so when I react a certain way to shit or say certain shit, I'm speaking out of love, you feel me?"

"All I know is, you called me a skank whore, so save all that nice talk, mister," Jewel said with a smile.

"So you accept my apology then?"

Jewel nodded her head and walked off.

I watched her sexy frame making its way back to my bedroom, and I couldn't resist. "I'm coming up there to take a shower with you. Don't make the water too hot."

Jewel turned and looked at me. She sucked her teeth and smiled. "Anyway."

Little did she know, I was dead-ass serious.

Chapter 16

"Lovers and Friends"

Jewel

My heart dropped when the shower curtain pulled back and a naked Touch stood before me. I didn't know if I should cover my body or turn my head from looking at his body. This was totally unlike him, and I was wondering where this was coming from. There'd been times when I got so drunk from the club that he would bathe me and then put me to bed, but that was back in the day, and he had never been naked with me.

As he stepped into the shower with me like it was nothing, I screamed, "Touch, no!"

"Chill out, girl. It ain't nothing but a shower." He reached for his Irish Spring body wash.

Oh well, I guess he's right, I thought to myself, feeling a little silly for reacting like a little schoolgirl. I studied Touch's physique as he washed his face beneath the running water from the showerhead. Damn, was he fine! Plus, his package was just right.

Touch caught me checking him out. "I see you looking."

"Boy, ain't nobody looking at you," I lied, embarrassed that he'd actually caught me.

I rushed to wash the blood out of my hair from my head wound. Then I went on to wash my body. I noticed that Touch's whole demeanor was kind of nonchalant the entire time we showered. Don't get me wrong, I didn't expect him to be jumping on top of me and trying to rape me or anything, but damn, a nigga should at least be trying to get a peep in. There was no way I was goin' to have this nigga around me, fronting like he didn't want to touch me, so I thought I might break the ice a little bit.

"Can you wash my back?" I said, hoping to get a little attention from Touch.

"Nope. How you wash yourself all the other times when you're showering alone?" he said playfully.

"Boy, don't play with me. You do me, and I'll do you." I handed him my washcloth.

I don't know if I was tripping or what, but as soon as he placed the towel on my back, it sent chills down my spine, and with every stroke, a sensation was sent throughout my body. Just as I was getting into it, it was over.

"My turn." Touch handed me my washcloth then grabbed for his.

"Turn around." I grabbed his towel and instructed him to turn his back to me.

"Nah, you said you were gonna do me." Touch looked at me with a straight face.

"No, silly. You know gotdamn well ain't nobody talking about *doing* you! I was talking about you wash my back, and I'll wash yours. Now turn around!" I demanded.

"Nah. Do it this way. I don't want you looking at my ass." Touch laughed.

I didn't even have the energy to fight with his crazy ass, so I just wrapped my arms around him, as though I was giving him a hug, and tried my best to wash his back thoroughly.

Touch wrapped his arms around me and squeezed me tight, like he was going to war and this was the last time he would see me.

It kinda caught me off guard, so I paused and looked up at him. We locked eyes as he looked down at me with those big brown eyes that I thought made him irresistible.

Then, in one motion, he slid his hands behind my neck, forcing it back, and slipped his tongue inside my mouth.

I didn't resist the least bit. It felt so right. We kissed with so much passion that the fire inside me was burning hot, and I was prepared to take it all the way. I moved my hand toward Touch's penis, but he stopped me.

"I love you, girl," he said as he grabbed his bath towel and stepped out of the shower.

I stood in the shower alone and speechless. This was all taking me by complete surprise. Touch and I had been friends for forever, and not once, through all the assumptions and innuendo, did we or, at least, did I ever think that we could be more than friends. But in the last twenty minutes all of that had changed. Years of friendship had changed. Where did that leave us now?

Baffled, I finished up my shower, hopped out, dried off, and baby-oiled my body. I threw on Touch's jersey and then met him in the living room.

"I'm hungry," I said, trying to forget the awkward moment we'd just shared.

"Wanna order Chinese?"

"Sure." I grabbed the phone then shuffled through his junk drawer in search of a Chinese menu.

Once I found one, I ordered our food then flopped down on the couch beside him. I took the remote from him and started to flip through his cable's On Demand, to find a movie for us to watch. By the time we'd flipped through six or seven movies and watched the previews and bullshitted with each other for a while, our food had arrived. We made ourselves comfortable on the sofa and ate Chinese as we watched the movie *Halloween*.

Not a fan of horror movies, I balled up underneath Touch's arm and lay my head on his chest, my feet across his lap. With what I had been through, being pistol-whipped and all, this was the safest that I had felt since the ordeal.

Although most of the movie was spent with me closing my eyes, screaming and jumping, I was still able to catch Touch constantly staring at me. Tired of wondering what the hell was on his mind, I just spat it out.

"Why the hell you keep looking at me?"

Instantly becoming irrated by my question, Touch sighed heavily and said, "This is some bullshit." He then quickly got up from the couch and headed toward the kitchen.

I followed hot on his heels, yelling, "What? What the fuck is your problem?" *I know this nigga ain't sitting up here thinking about that shit between me and Calico.* I stared all up in Touch's face, waiting for an answer, but he didn't respond. He just shook his head and stared at me.

"So what? You think I'm pitiful now? That's why you shaking your head?"

"You have no idea, Jewel. I need to be with you, not that nigga Calico. That muthafucka almost got you raped. Maybe killed. All these years, and not once did you think to look my way, but this new nigga come into town and give you some money, now you ready to go down for his bullshit. I have protected you and cared about you all this time, and now you asking me some dumb shit? You know what? You right. You are pitiful because you here tellin' me I need a good woman and you can't see that you're it."

This was the second time tonight that Touch left me

speechless. I just never knew that he felt this way. I mean, sure, he was fine as hell, but he had Ciara and the fat rats. Besides, Touch couldn't be some random nigga I put on my team. I would dismiss the whole squad just to be with him.

My thoughts were interrupted when I heard moving around.

"I need to step out for minute." Touch grabbed his keys and headed toward the front door.

I raced in front of him and stood in front of the door like a club security guard. "You ain't going outta this house, Touch," I yelled, tears of frustration welling up in my eyes.

"You want me to stay?" he asked calmly.

"Yes."

"You sure?"

"Yes."

"You don't know what you're asking for, Jewel."

"Yes, I definitely know what I'm asking for. Just don't leave me. Please, don't leave."

Touch grabbed me by my throat, startling me. The pressure from his hand pinned my head against the front door. He pressed his body against mine, and began to kiss me passionately again, causing my pussy to get wet within seconds. He released my neck and used his leg to force my thighs slightly open. I could feel the solidness of his dick through his boxers as the force from his body pressed against mine. With each hand he gripped my outer thighs and lifted me off the floor.

Eager to have him inside me, I wrapped my legs around his waist. In only a matter of seconds, I had lifted Touch's jersey over my head, and he'd dropped his boxers. And in one big thrust, he was inside of me, fulfilling my every desire. I didn't say a word as he forced his manhood deep inside of me. Not only did my body yearn for more, but so did my heart. I wanted Touch.

For the first time, I'd felt that chemistry between man and woman that I'd heard so much about. It was surreal. I was reaching my peak so fast.

"Cum with me, Touch," I whispered in his ear, and like magic, we both came together.

Once again tears ran from my eyes, but this time they weren't tears of fear. They were tears of ultimate satisfaction.

After a session like that, there was nothing else left to do but wash up, and go to bed. And in Touch's case, take a smoke, wash up, and go to bed.

The next morning, I was awakened by a call from Sasha. "Hello?" I answered full of attitude.

"What's wrong with you?"

"Nothing now, but when there was a problem, you sure didn't answer your damn cell phone." I was still pissed that Sasha didn't answer her phone when I'd called her the other night.

"I'm sorry, Jewel. I worked late that night, and I was fucked-up when I left the club. Are you okay?"

"Well, I am now," I said, full of disgust.

"So what happened?"

"To make a long story short, me and Calico got arrested when we were leaving the strip club."

"Oh, you went to see your little bitch, Paradise, huh?" Sasha interrupted my story with her regular bullshit, totally overlooking the fact that I said I'd gotten locked up.

"Like I was saying, I spent a few hours in jail but was released on bond. Calico is still in there. Then after that some niggas ran up in my shit and pistol-whipped me."

"Oh my God! Jewel, are you sure you're okay? Where are you now?"

"I'm at Touch's house." I smiled to myself.

"Oh, for real. What he doing?"

"Sleeping. I put that ass to sleep."

"What?"

"Bitch, you heard me—I put that ass to sleep!"

Sasha said in a tone of disapproval, "Jewel, don't tell me you fucked Touch."

"I sure did."

"But that's your best friend. I thought you would never go there with him. I hope this is not another one of your money schemes, 'cause if it is, it sounds pretty pathetic to me. Oh, let me guess, you gonna use Touch now because Calico is locked up. Jewel, that is foul."

Usually I can take Sasha's jealous rants, but today was different. She went on and on, like Touch was her fucking blood brother or some shit.

"Relax. It's not even like that. And why do you care anyway? I had no ulterior motive when we had sex. And the thing about it is that it felt so right. For the first time I have true feelings for a nigga. It's like he's my soul mate, and to think he was right in my face the whole damn time."

"Whatever. Well, I gotta go. I have another call coming in." Sasha hung up the phone before I could even say goodbye.

That was definitely new for her. She had never hung up on me like that before. *What's her problem with me seeing Touch anyway?*

No sooner than she hung up, my phone rang again. This time it was a number I didn't recognize. My first instinct was to not even answer, but I went against it. "Hello?" I answered with caution.

I heard a woman's voice say, "Hold on," then Calico chimed in.

"Calico!" I screamed, waking Touch.

"Hey, baby. Look, I don't have much time. I'm on a three-way, so listen carefully."

Although I wanted to blast him about that shit that happened the day before, I gave him an opportunity to speak first. I listened attentively as Calico explained he was granted a million dollars bail, and was going to pay the ten percent of that, one hundred thousand dollars, in cash and bond out. He also told me that he needed me to collect one hundred fifty thousand dollars that Touch owed him. Once received, some of the money was to be given to his attorney as a retainer, and I was to hold on to the rest, which he would need to make moves when he hit the streets.

"Okay, I got it, and I'm on it as soon as we get off the phone. Now let me share a few things with you," I said calmly.

I spent the next five minutes giving Calico a rushed version of how that nigga Sincere came up in my house. But with the automated voice counting down the minutes and with Touch constantly yelling at me in the background to hang up the phone, I just couldn't deliver like I wanted to.

Thankfully Calico had a bond, so he would be out, and as soon as he was, I would be the first to snap off on his ass.

Before I could even properly hang up the phone, Touch said, "Yo, you insist on dealing with that nigga, huh?"

"Touch, I just want to let him know what's going on and wrap things up. Once things are in order, I'm gonna back away. I just don't want to up and turn my back on him, not right now anyway. Right now, I'm all he has."

"So you think," Touch mumbled. "Trust me, that nigga got plenty of other chicks playing the same position as you." He got out of the bed and stood up and looked at the missed calls on his cell phone.

"Oh, and he wants you to give me the one hundred and

fifty grand you owe him. I have to pay his lawyer with a portion of that."

"Yeah, okay. Whatever." Touch headed into the bathroom and closed the door behind him.

All I could do was shake my head. I damn sure didn't need no more stress in my life.

Chapter 17

"Opportunity Knocks"

Sasha

I so didn't feel like answering my phone when I saw Jewel's name pop up on my caller ID, but since she had called me four times in a row, I decided to pick up.

I answered the phone with a sarcastic attitude, "Either you're a psycho bitch, or you're a stalker. Which one is it?"

"Sasha, what is your problem?" Jewel asked.

I wanted to tell her that I was tired of her bullshit, tired of her always flaunting shit and showing off, tired of her always making a come-up, while I was in a unending state of struggling to get mine. Instead, I kept my mouth shut. It had been about three days since I had abruptly hung up the phone on her, and to be honest, I had absolutely no intentions of ever calling her ass back.

"Helloooo."

"Yeah, I'm here. You called me. So what do you want?"

Jewel blew some air into the phone, as if she had a reason to have an attitude. "Look, I know you been going through some shit lately, and to be honest, I'm sensing something, like you have a problem with me or some shit—"

"Well, actually—" I cut Jewel off, ready to cuss her ass out and tell her to leave me the fuck alone, but then she interrupted me just as quickly.

"Wait! Would you just hear me out and let me finish?"

I kept quiet.

"What I was trying to say was that I got my hands on some money and I'm gonna be heading to New York to go shopping. I wanted to do something nice for you and have you come with me. My treat, all expenses paid."

"Damn, that must be some killer-ass pussy!" I couldn't resist making a smart comment. "So how much did you get Touch for?"

"Sasha, what the fuck is your problem? I call you with regular everyday shit, and you got an attitude. I call you trying to be nice, and you still got an attitude. I don't get it. Is it that time of the month or something?"

"You don't get it because you're not me and you ain't going through the shit that I'm going through."

"Yeah, but, Sasha, I'm your homegirl. You can tell me what's going on without taking things out on me. You already know that I'll be there for you and look out for you in any way that I can."

"Blah, blah, blah, blah," was what I felt like saying to Jewel, but I was no dummy. I was at least gonna get a free trip to New York and get some clothes in the process, so I held my tongue.

"So how much money did you get your hands on?"

"Well, Touch gave me one hundred and fifty grand."

"A hundred and fifty gees?"

"Bitch, dry your panties off, 'cause the shit ain't my money. Some of the money is supposed to go to pay Calico's lawyer, and the rest is going to Calico. It's just money that Touch owed him. But, the way I see it, ten percent of that has to go to me as a fee for my services. You know how I do."

Regardless of my attitude with Jewel, I couldn't help but

laugh at her. I had to admit, I loved the way she got down, especially when my ass could benefit from it.

"Jewel, you are a true hot-ass mess."

Jewel laughed. "Nah, that shit is only right. It's a ten percent facilitation fee."

"Hooker, your ass can't even spell *facilitation*."

Jewel and I both laughed. Then she told me that she was gonna book my ticket and call me back with the details.

"So we good now?" she asked me.

"No, I'm still gonna fight you when I see you," I said jokingly.

Yeah, I switched up and went into a joking mood, but the truth of the matter was, I was just fronting my ass off. Jewel had her hands on one hundred fifty grand that I was gonna help her spend. As far as I was concerned, that was one hundred fifty thousand reasons for me to put on an acting performance.

Right after I hung up the phone, I sat straight up in my bed. My mind was registering what she really said. Then, suddenly I had an idea.

That bitch said she has her hands on one hundred fifty grand. Sasha, if you put on an Oscar award winning performance, you can leave New York and come back to ATL with at least one hundred thousand, I thought to myself. This was definitely it. It was time for my come-up. My panties really were getting wet just thinking about what I would do with a hundred thousand dollars.

I got up from out of my bed and paced back and forth in my room, trying my hardest to think of just what I was gonna say to her, and how I was gonna say it, for her to hit me off with that money. I just didn't know if I should call Jewel back and kick my game to her, or if I should wait until we got to New York to give her my sob story.

Jewel ran plenty of game, and I'd learned from the best.

It was time to give her a taste of her own medicine. I knew I had to be careful because one thing for sure is, game recognized game. Jewel was an all-star at this, so she couldn't be easily manipulated. My hands were tied. This wasn't gonna be an easy task.

Think, Sasha, think! I pleaded with myself.

After a few minutes, it came to me that when Jewel called me back I had to go in for the kill. I couldn't wait because, if I waited until we got to New York, she might divvy the money up by then and pay the lawyer and hit Calico off.

Yeah, bitch, I'm-a play your game. You think you the only one with that pot of gold between your legs that can fuck money outta any nigga, right?

I knew that I had some killer sex myself. A tongue and pussy that I knew Jewel would die over. That girl loved me and she knew it. And with one hundred thousand in cash, I was gonna make her prove it.

Chapter 18

"Back against the Wall"

Calico

As soon as I made bond, I made a few calls and had one of my chicks make arrangements to get me out. Then I headed straight to my attorney's office. I had been indicted on a Racketeer Influenced and Corrupt Organizations charge, better known as a RICO charge. Those fucking prosecutors were acting like I was John Gotti, talking all that organized crime bullshit. From what my lawyer was saying, the shit didn't look good. Her theory was that the state had a ninety-seven percent conviction rate on this type of charge, and that I had to seriously consider taking a plea deal. If not, I could be looking at twenty years.

"Fuck that!" I told my lawyer bluntly. "I ain't copping out to shit. And I ain't no snitch, so there's no way I'm cooperating. They can forget that."

My lawyer was a sexy, green-eyed, blonde-haired Italian supermodel-looking chick. Besides the fact that she was smart as shit, what I liked about her most was that she understood the struggle. Her pops used to be in organized crime and got locked up when she was eleven years old and had been in prison ever since. The fact that she had grown up without him led her to want to be a lawyer.

"Michael, you know I'll fight for you till the bitter end, but make no mistake about it, it's gonna be a dogfight to beat these charges."

"I only fuck with the best. That's why I got you," I said before leaving.

I had explained to her that Jewel would come by to give her one hundred and twenty-five thousand. And she made sure to remind me that I would be looking at, at least, one million in fees by the time it was all said and done. But I knew that it would be money well spent because she would have to hire investigators, expert witnesses, and shit like that, on my behalf. Once I wrapped that shit up, I was on the next flight home to California.

I'd been in California for the entire five days after seeing my lawyer. That shit with niggas running up in Jewel's crib really had me fucked up. I had put a hit out on Sincere, and things were immediately dealt with. But something still didn't sit right with me. I couldn't understand how these dudes knew where to find me and how much coke I had. I wasn't a sloppy dude, and nobody really knew I was kicking it with Jewel like that. I knew I needed to talk to her more about the situation.

Since my arrest I had refused to talk on my cell phone. Instead, I was only using prepaid cell phones that I would get rid of on a weekly basis. Just to be extra careful, I made sure that Jewel and other people that I spoke to on a regular basis didn't call me from one of their regular phone numbers.

"You know this prepaid cell phone shit is for the birds," Jewel complained to me.

"It's a slight inconvenience for freedomm baby," I explained to her. "Anyway, a couple of things real quick. I handled that shit with Sincere, just like I told you I would. Them fucking New York niggas think muthafuckas is just gonna get down or lay down 'cause they from New York. I guess niggas know different now."

"Oh shit! Yeah, I heard about that. I had no idea."

"One thing, though . . . shit don't seem right. It had to be someone else involved, or something more to it. I ain't tell no niggas I was chilling with you or how much shit I had. Tell me any and everything you can remember about these dudes. You sure you've never seen them before?" I asked, fishing for more information.

I listened attentively as Jewel spoke. I thought about everyone I'd come in contact with on that visit. Then it was one thing Jewel said that stuck out.

I made sure I'd heard correctly. "You said a chick told them I had coke in the house?"

"Yep."

"Say no more." I deaded that conversation.

I knew exactly who had set me up, and that bitch was to get dealt with next. Shit had finally come together. That shiesty bitch, Diana, was the only chick I'd dealt with that day, and I remembered seeing her hollering at two unfamiliar dudes in a car with New York tags as we were leaving the strip club. I didn't even bother telling Jewel.

"Now about this money, you hit my lawyer off yet?" I said, changing the subject.

"No, but—"

"Jewel, listen, this shit ain't a game. I don't want you walking around with that kind of bread. Now, you said you wanted to be my ride-or-die bitch. I need you to prove it to me. Take the shit to over to her today."

"Okay, okay, I'm on it."

"So what is Touch saying?"

"Saying about what?"

"That bitch-ass nigga, I'm surprised he ain't give you a hard time giving you my loot."

"Calico, what are you talking about? Why you calling him a bitch? And for the record, Touch gave me that money with no problem."

I didn't go any further with that issue. I really didn't have the time to concern myself with Touch. My money was getting low, and I had to get my weight up. Those New York niggas had been coming down to Virginia and trying to supply the same market that I was supplying, and now I knew how. I was sure that trick-ass Diana was making it real easy for those niggas, putting them on to my customers and everything.

I admit that they had caught me slippin', and in the process, my money took a hit. It was nothing that I couldn't recover from, but I was experiencing a slight drought. And with that case that I had caught, it just seemed like the government and my competition smelled blood, and were moving in for the kill.

My back was starting to feel like it was up against the wall, but one thing about me was, I knew I was smarter than all the street niggas out there. And I was never the one to back down from shit. I was gonna lay low for a month or two in California and let things run their course, but I was definitely gonna be plotting shit out in the meantime. I ran Virginia. That's how it was, and that's how shit was gonna continue to be.

When I hung up the phone with Jewel, I poured myself a glass of Hennessy on the rocks and sparked a blunt that I had rolled earlier. I took the remote to my CD player, and I turned on the *American Gangster* soundtrack and went right to track 10 and blasted the song "Ignorant Shit." In seconds

the lyrics had me amped as I took pulls from the weed. I
turned the volume up even louder as I drank from my glass
and recited along with the song.

My head was feeling nice. It was like, instantly, I could
care less about my legal problems or anything else as I continued to rap out loud as if I was Jay-Z.

Chapter 19

"Money Scam"

Jewel

"Hey, Boobie!" I yelled as I raced toward Sasha, who was standing at the luggage carousel at the airport.

"Hey, baby!" She rushed into my arms, and I hugged her tight as she wrapped her arms around me and grabbed a handful of each of my butt cheeks and squeezed them tight.

I quickly removed her hands. "Sasha, we're in the airport. People are watching."

Laughing, Sasha grabbed her bag from her incoming flight from Atlanta, and we chatted as we walked to the counter to check in for our flight to New York.

Sasha asked about the discussion we'd had about flipping Calico's money the previous day. "So you reach a decision yet?"

"Yeah, I have. I ain't gon' lie, that shit sounds like a good idea. I'm just thinking about the risk," I said to Sasha, even though my gut was telling me to just look at Sasha's loser track record and to not go through with her grand money plans.

Sasha tried to assure me that her plan was foolproof. "What risk? Diablo is your homeboy. He loves you to death. You know he'll give you the product at a good-ass price. And you don't have to worry about a driver. I'll drive to Atlanta with the money and bring the shit back up here to you. Baby, there is no risk. You have nothing to lose."

I flipped through my Gucci handbag, trying to locate my driver's license so that I could hand it to the clerk at the airline counter. "Yeah, I hear you, but Calico is on my ass about paying his lawyer."

"Just stall him, or better yet, just lie and say you paid the lawyer. What the fuck? Girl, don't act like you don't know how to game a nigga."

I looked at Sasha, just as the clerk handed me my boarding pass. "See, that's the thing, Sasha. This ain't a game. Calico is really going through it right now, and I can't fuck his money up."

"You won't fuck it up, Jewel. We got this, trust me."

Purposely ignoring Sasha and not responding to her on that issue, I walked toward Starbucks so I could get a grande caramel frappuccino. I asked her, "You want something from Starbucks?"

Sasha shook her head no, and then she gave me this look, as if to check me for not answering her. "Jewel?"

Sasha looked so irresistibly cute, and she did have one helluva plan. Besides, a bitch could always use some extra dough, but I didn't want to just give in to her right there on the spot. This was no ordinary nigga I was going to game. This was the "California Connection." Shit could get really messy if this plan of hers wasn't executed properly.

"Let me think a little more. I'll let you know by the end of our little trip.

Right now, all we need to be thinking about is spending this fifteen gees!"

* * *

The plane ride was quick. Sasha and I both slept through the whole flight into New York's LaGuardia Airport.

"Come this way." I instructed Sasha to follow me as we exited the plane, and I headed toward the limousine driver that was holding a sign that read C. Diaz.

"Damn, you doing it big, huh?"

"Yeah, I'm doing it big, but not on my dollar. I also have a little business to take care of while I'm out here."

"Business?" Sasha responded full of attitude.

I knew how salt jealous Sasha could be, and that was why I had purposely held back from telling her about the other reason for my trip to New York.

"Relax. It's only a quick meeting. This independent hip-hop record label that I've done some ghostwriting work for in the past referred me to this major publishing company here in New York. They want me to do some work on this book that TMF is putting out."

"TMF? Bitch, shut up!" Sasha yelled.

I knew Sasha would be impressed with those niggas. Who wouldn't be? TMF stood for True Mafia Family. It was a group of niggas that had just as much drugs, money, and power as the Italian mafia. They had the same organization and success as the Italians, but all these dudes were black. There were the Frank Lucas of their time.

"Yep. I'm just gon' run in there and meet with everyone, see what they talking about, and sign my name on the dotted line."

Chapter 20

"Temperatures Rising"

Touch

"So y'all doing it big up there in New York," I said to Jewel, practically shouting into the phone in an attempt to compete with all the noise in the background.

"Yeah, we met with the publisher, and I got the contract. I signed off on that shit, which I probably shouldn't have done without having a lawyer look at it. But, hey, fuck it, the dollars look right."

There was so much noise and commotion behind Jewel, I could barely make out two words of this conversation.

"We hanging out and I'm trying to get to know these niggas so I can write from their point of view. But I'll call you as soon as we get back to Virginia."

"A'ight, but one thing. I really called to ask you why the fuck is Calico calling and questioning me about his bread? You paid his lawyer right?"

"Touch, come on now, that bitch got her money, so if Calico is saying different, you tell him to call me."

"Enough said."

Jewel hung up the phone, and my next call was to Calico. He didn't pick up, but I let him know that I had verified with Jewel that she'd paid the lawyer and that I didn't appreciate his bitch ass calling me and insinuating that I was trying to play with his money.

The truth of the matter, though, was that I knew Jewel was bullshitting. I knew that she hadn't paid that lawyer. Now, exactly why she hadn't paid the lawyer and what she was planning on doing with Calico's money, I didn't know, and to be honest, I really didn't give a fuck. That was on Calico for trying to run game on a chick like Jewel. But one thing I did know was if that nigga ever tried to come at Jewel sideways, I would be the first to deal with his ass. And it wouldn't be a hit. That one I would have to handle face to face, because then it would be personal.

My baby moms was back to stressing me the fuck out. I was going to see her, so I could check that ass for some smart comments she'd made. This bitch had to nerve to say some shit about me not fucking her and that Calico was the only dude that knew how to fuck her like she wanted to be fucked. A broad can say anything on the phone, but shit is different when you up in their face. I was going to her crib, to prove that shit.

She knew how I felt about her fucking these cats out here in the streets. That's why I wasn't with her bitch ass anymore. If she really fucked Calico, I would lose my mine. I would really kill that bitch. She was the mother of my kids, yeah, that's true, but that wouldn't make a damn difference if she was even halfway telling me the truth. The way I was feeling about her and Calico lately, shit wasn't looking good for either of them, as far as I was concerned.

Chapter 21

"Seal the Deal"

Sasha

"Oh my God," I said as I opened my eyes and slowly sat up in the bed. A night of club-hopping with TMF had taken a toll on me. I was definitely feeling the effects of the Ace of Spades champagne I'd drank the night before. Or should I say Armand de Brignac, since Jewel's bourgeoisie ass kept reminding me of the proper name the entire damn night.

My head was spinning as I tried to focus my eyes to see the time on the clock. It was twelve o'clock, three hours before our flight. That left me roughly an hour and a half to give Jewel a little sexual persuasion so that this plan to flip Calico's money could happen.

Without waking Jewel, I ordered breakfast for us and had room service deliver it. Then I woke her to breakfast in bed.

"Thank you, baby," she said in a groggy morning tone.

"No. Thank you for such a wonderful trip," I said sweetly. Then I kissed her.

After we ate our food, I put the tray outside the door. Jewel was full and content as she sat in bed and flipped through channels on the television. Now it was time to bring up the money.

"So, baby, did you decide anything yet?" I asked as I lay beside her, my leg over hers.

"Well, I'm still not sure. Don't get me wrong, it sounds like a hell of a plan, and everything you're saying makes sense, but I'm still unsure."

"It's okay," I said, knowing I was about to do exactly what it took to make her confident.

I lay my head on the pillow next to Jewel and watched TV as she fell back asleep. Once she was sound asleep, I gently straddled her naked body without saying a word. With a feather-like touch, I lightly circled the outline of her nipple with my tongue then gave them small sporadic suckles combined with light nibbles.

Jewel moaned with pleasure as I slowly crept down her stomach, leaving a row of kisses on the way. Reaching her womanhood, I slid my tongue over her lips and even in her hole, purposely avoiding her clit. I sucked each lip separately, giving them special attention and heightening her desire even more.

Jewel moaned again and began to thrust her hips forward as she pushed her fingers between the tight curls of my hair and grasped the back of my head. This was a sure indication she wanted more.

Satisfied that she'd reach optimum levels of desire, I finally moved toward her clit. Using only my lips and tongue, I began to suck her pleasure zone.

Jewel moaned even louder, and her thrust became constant and more intense as she reached her peak.

Ready to send her over the edge, I shoved my middle finger and my ring finger inside her, certain to hit her G-spot, but sure not to disrupt the ultimate clit massage she was receiving. Moments later, like milk from a baby's bottle, her wetness flowed, and I drank.

I lifted my head from between Jewel's legs, my face still

wet from her explosion. I asked her, "Are you certain about that money scheme yet?"

She laughed. "How could anyone say no to a face like that?"

"My thoughts exactly!"

"We'll do exactly as you said. When we get back to Virginia, I'll give you the money, and you can go meet Diablo."

"Perfect choice. Now we about to see some real money and do some real big things. Fuck niggas! Get money!"

We gave each other a high-five.

Or, in my case, fuck bitches! Get money! I then began to chant that verse of the song as I walked to the bathroom to get cleaned up. Cheesing from ear to ear, I was about to do me.

Chapter 22

"Don't Test Me"

Calico

I asked my right-hand man, "So you sure that bitch never came home?"

"The muthafuckin' mail in her mailbox is piled up and shit, no lights ever on at the crib, and ain't no noise coming from the house. That bitch ain't there. I sat on her block 'round the clock."

"What about her ride?"

"I don't see that shit. I been to all the spots. I seen Touch on occasion here and there, but she was never with that dude. I don't know what to tell you."

I ended my conversation with my homeboy who I had sent from California to Virginia so that he could locate Jewel, see what was the deal with my dough. Just like a scheming trick, Jewel wasn't nowhere to be found.

"Fuck!" I screamed. I stood up and punched a hole into the wall of my bedroom.

I repeatedly called Jewel's cell phone, but she wasn't picking up. I called from block numbers and unblocked numbers, but it didn't make a difference. She was definitely ducking me. I knew that was the reason why she was screening her calls. I called one last time, determined that this was gonna be the last time that I called that bitch.

"Jewel, I don't know what kinda shit you on, or who the fuck you think you dealing with, but understand this, at this point, shit ain't even about the money, this shit is about being disrespected. Don't think that just because I fucked you that I won't personally murder your ass."

I ended the call, getting more and more vexed by the second.

It didn't make no sense on harping on the shit, because I still had a lot of moves to make, and other shit to stay on top of. One thing was for sure, in the end, if that bitch didn't come through, her little pretty ass was definitely gonna pay.

I was planning on meeting one of my new lieutenants named Poppo at Roscoe's Chicken and Waffles. Since so much heat was on me and the people close to me, I felt that it would be smart to start adding new layers of people between myself and those I was doing business with. So my plan was to start grooming Poppo, who I trusted the most, to handle shit for me in Virginia, and that was what we were gonna be meeting at Roscoe's to discuss.

While I was driving toward Roscoe's, my cell phone rang. I noticed the caller ID had a 757 number on it. I answered the phone, "Yo."

"Calico?"

"Yo, who dis?"

"It's Jewel."

I immediately pulled my car over to the curb so I could speak to that bitch with no distractions.

"You got some big-ass balls, Jewel. You do know that, right?"

"Oh my God! Calico, what are you talking about? I heard

the message that you just left me, and I'm like, 'What the fuck is going on?' "

"Jewel, let's not play this fucking game, a'ight? 'Cause I swear that if I was next to you right now I would choke the shit out your little gold-digging ass!"

Jewel was silent and didn't say shit. All I heard her do was sigh into the phone.

"Jewel, where the fuck is my money?"

"I paid that shit to your lawyer. Ask her where the fuck your money is. I really don't need this bullshit, Calico."

"Your ass is still talking shady? Yeah, a'ight. You and Touch can stay on that snake shit if y'all want to, but on the real, y'all are fucking with the wrong dude."

"Call that bitch right now."

"Call who?"

"Your fucking lawyer. Three-way her ass, 'cause I wanna hear her say she ain't get that money. I know who I paid the fucking money to."

I was definitely not in the mood for no bullshit games. "Jewel, I ain't fucking calling nobody, 'cause you full of shit. You been ducking my calls, not calling me—"

Jewel cut me off in mid-sentence. "What the hell are you talking about? I was out of town in New York on business, so I didn't have time to call you back."

"What fucking business?"

"Ghostwriting business."

"You full of shit!"

"Oh, so now I wasn't outta town? Calico, I can fax you the contract that I went out there to sign."

I didn't respond to Jewel.

"So now you don't want to call her. Look, I'm telling you to call the lawyer, so I can hear what this bitch is saying. Now, if you don't want to call her, then that shit is on you.

But you better stop blowing up my phone about this bull-shit."

"Test me if you want to, Jewel. Keep tryin' my patience. That's all I'm telling you. And you can tell Touch the exact same thing. You think this shit is funny? Some fuckin' play-time because you wanna pretend to act all hood and shit? Okay, let's see who's having fun after I'm done with yo' ass."

With that said, I hung up the phone. I knew there was no need for me to three-way Jewel into my lawyer's office. I had already paid my lawyer the money that I owed her. I paid her that shit out of my pocket, not out of the money that Jewel and Touch were trying to play me for. And I knew that there was no way in hell that my lawyer would ever try to get over on me about no money issues.

But, like I had said, Jewel and Touch could test me if they wanted to. They were definitely fucking with the wrong cat, 'cause I wasn't the one to be fucked with. My temper was rising, and my revenge list was getting longer by the day. Niggas and bitches alike were beginning to take me for a pussy, and it was time I started to make an example out of someone.

Chapter 23

"Label Me Ike Turner"

Touch

I couldn't find Ciara anywhere. Just like her bum-ass friends, her lazy ass wasn't ever about getting off her ass and doing shit. I knew there was only one place that she could be, and that was at her homegirl Monica's house. Sure enough, when I pulled up to Monica's house, Ciara's car was parked in the driveway.

After parking my car in the middle of the street, I jumped out and went to Monica's front door and started ringing the bell like a madman. I wasn't a short-tempered kind of dude. In fact, I had a real long fuse, and I definitely wasn't one to be hitting on no chicks. That wasn't me at all. But with certain bad memories continuing to flashback in my mind, something had snapped. I knew that I was about to cross that line to "woman-beater" status. I was trying to keep the thoughts out of my head, but I was having no such luck.

Even as I rang Monica's doorbell, I continued to have flashbacks of Ciara fucking one of my workers when I was locked up. My flashbacks continued, as I was reminded of the night I came home and my girl had burned my money and bleached my furs.

Then I was reminded of that phone call I got when Jewel was fucking Calico. My otherwise easygoing nature was gone, leaving me with an anger that I'd never experienced before. I was literally looking to fuck a bitch up, and there was one just behind this door that needed that serious-ass beating.

A voice from the inside asked, "Who is it?"

"It's Touch."

After I said my name, everything went silent for a few moments. Then I heard some rumbling around inside before the door flung open to reveal Ciara standing there in her bare feet, jeans, and a top. She was drinking a Heineken, and in the background, I could hear Judge Mathis on the television.

Ciara looked me up and down. She didn't say anything, but her body language was screaming, "What the fuck do you want?" She then took a swig of her beer.

Looking at her ghettoness just disgusted the shit out of me. I couldn't help but slap that beer right out of her hands.

With no other words being said, Ciara just went crazy and started swinging on me like she was the female heavyweight champ Laila Ali. "You don't be coming in here like you own the place, tryin' to put your fucking hands on me!" she barked, landing punches and scratches to my face, chest, and arms.

I hauled back with one right hook to her jaw, sending her straight to the floor like a rag doll. I immediately put my foot on her neck and applied as much pressure as I absolutely could, hoping to snap that shit in half.

"Ciara, I'm asking you one time—Did you fuck that nigga?"

Just as I said that, Monica came charging at me with a

steak knife. Luckily, I saw her just in time and side-stepped her and grabbed hold of her wrist and bent it all the way back. She screamed out in pain and dropped the knife.

"Ahhh shit!" I screamed as I looked down and realized that my baby mother had just stabbed me in my calf with the broken Heineken bottle. "You fucking bitch!" I yelled. I kicked her in her mouth and proceeded to stomp both her and Monica right there in Monica's doorway. There were no words for the pain I was feeling, but there were many in between all the blows I was inflicting.

Apparently we had been making so much noise that one of Monica's neighbors came running over to see what was going.

I hollered, "This ain't none of your fucking business, miss! We all right. Everything is all right!" and slammed the front door shut.

I picked Ciara up off the ground and flung her across the room, and when I caught up with her, I grabbed her by her hair and punched on her like she was a human punching bag.

Meanwhile, Monica was still on the floor, clutching her wrist and writhing in pain.

"Did you fuck Calico?"

Ciara looked at me with the little bit of energy she had left. She looked as if she was trying to spit on me, but the only thing that came out of her mouth was blood. Through her tears and ragged look, she said, "You're such an insecure pussy. Maybe if you weren't fucking Diana, I wouldn't have fucked Calico."

I looked at Ciara in disbelief, wondering how the fuck she knew I'd fuck Diana.

"Look at you, looking all stupid in the face. Yeah, that's right. Your boy told me. Calico told me all about your little sexcapade with that trick. And after a smack in the face like that, all I could do was fuck the nigga. He laid it on me so damn good. I knew it was worth it."

At that point, I sort of snapped out of the rage that I'd slipped into. My leg was stinging like a bitch. I looked down and saw a patch of blood staining my pants, and there was blood all over my sneakers.

"Yeah, I fucked him! And he wasn't no weak-dick nigga like your ass! What you need to be doing is watching your back, muthafucka!" She tried to laugh, but coughed up blood. "From what I'm hearin' in the streets, you a snitch, and Calico is gonna git you." Ciara had enough energy for that last sentence then she passed out.

A neighbor burst open the front door and came inside the house. "Monica, you okay? I already called the cops. They should be here soon."

I looked over at Ciara and started to get angry at her ghetto ass again, but thankfully my rage had subsided enough to limp out of the house, jump in my car, and pull off.

Before I could make it home, both Sasha and Jewel began taking turns blowing up my cell phone. I really didn't want to speak to either one of them, or to anybody for that matter, so I let all of my calls go to voice mail as I continued on home.

I went straight to my bathroom and applied rubbing alcohol to the gash on my calf that Ciara had caused. "Uggghhhh!"

Sasha had stopped calling me, but Jewel was continuing to blow up my phone.

Through my pain, I finally decided to answer.

"Jewel, what's up?" I asked through clenched teeth.

"Damn, Touch, you sound like you taking a shit or something," Jewel said.

"Nah, that fucking bitch Ciara cut my ass."

"What? When did this happen?"

I went on to explain everything to Jewel, and she made me describe the cut to her.

"Can you see the white meat?"

"Hell, yeah. I see white meat, red meat, and some blue stringy shit."

"Oh Lord! Touch, you ain't gonna patch that shit up with no Band-Aid. I can tell you that right now. You need to take your ass to the emergency room and get stitched up."

I looked at the three blood-drenched towels that I had used to try and stop the flow of blood coming from my cut and realized that Jewel was probably right. "I think you right."

"Okay, so you going now?"

"Yeah."

"Which hospital you going to? I'll meet you over there."

"Sentara Leigh."

"Okay, I'm on my way. Wrap your leg as tight as you can with a T-Shirt or some shit before you leave the house, a'ight? I'll be there as soon as I can," Jewel said to me and then hung up the phone.

When I made it to the emergency room, I saw that it was crowded. I figured that I might have to wait for a while, but after I gave the nurse all of my personal information, she came from around her desk and took a quick look at my cut. After examining it for about thirty seconds, she ushered me right into the back where all of the other nurses and doctors were tending to patients.

"That was quick." I smiled. "You letting me skip all those people out there?"

"Well, I'm not sure, it looks like you may have severed muscle tissue. I don't want to have you wait out there for too long and take a chance on you properly using the leg ever again."

I thought about my baby mother. *I'm-a kill that bitch!* I followed the nurse, until she situated me in one of the rooms. She told me, "Sit on the bed. A doctor would be right with you."

Thankfully, after fifteen minutes or so, a doctor examined me and determined that although the wound was deep, it didn't affect muscle tissue. "It it was awfully close. We'll get you stitched up and out of here within a half an hour or so."

I nodded my head in agreement. I then lay back on the bed, propped my head up on the pillow, and stared into space. My quiet was then interrupted by my annoying-ass ringtone.

"Leave me alone. Shit!" I looked down at my cell phone and saw Sasha's number pop up. "Hello?"

"Touch, it's Sasha."

"Yeah, I know that, Sasha. What's up?"

Sasha sucked her teeth. "See, I knew it. So it was just about some pussy, right? So you just fuck and buck, Touch? Now you done hit it, you don't give a fuck."

I didn't say anything.

"Uh, sir, I'm afraid you can't use the cell phone in the hospital," a nurse said to me.

Thank God. Saved by the nurse, I thought.

"Sasha, listen, I'm in the hospital right now and I can't talk, but I'll call you back."

"Yeah, whateva." Sasha abruptly hung up.

"I'm sorry about that," I said to the nurse as I put my phone away.

No sooner than I had put my phone away, Jewel came walking into my room.

"Hey, pookie face," she said as she walked up to me and gave me a kiss on the cheek.

Jewel was looking good as hell. My dick got hard instantly, just looking at her divalicious self. At that moment, I realized I was actually playing myself by giving a fuck what my baby mother did, and for giving two shits about Sasha and how she felt. I realized that Jewel had everything I wanted and needed in a woman. I knew that I had to make her my girl and that we had to move forward in some type of commitment shit.

"You okay?" Jewel asked.

I looked down at her peep-toe stiletto heels. "Damn, them some sexy-ass shoes."

"I got these when I went to New York." Jewel smiled. "You like 'em, huh?"

Before I could even reply to Jewel, two police officers walked into my room.

"Trayvon Davis?" they asked.

I attempted to sit up as straight as I could. "Yeah, that's me. What's up?"

"Just relax, sir," one of the cops said to me.

One cop went on one side of my bed, and the other cop went to the other side. Each cop grabbed one of my arms and placed a handcuff on each wrist and then proceeded to also cuff the railing of the bed that I was sitting on.

"What the fuck is this?" I yelled.

"Trayvon Davis, we're placing you under arrest. You have the right to remain silent. Anything you say can and will be used . . ."

This is some bullshit! I said to myself as the cop continued to read me my rights. I don't know why, but just then a nervous smirk came across my face.

Chapter 24

"My Time to Shine"

Sasha

When I got back to Atlanta with the hundred thousand dollars, I knew one thing and one thing only. Sasha was going to do whatever the fuck Sasha felt like doing. If I didn't feel like doing shit for the day, then I wasn't doing shit. If I felt like buying new clothes every day, then that's what the hell I was going to do.

As I sat in my bedroom and counted the most money that I'd ever had at one time, I knew that I wasn't going back to Bottoms Up. Fuck that dancer life! I was tired of that shit, tired of the hustle. Tired of lame-ass, crusty-ass niggas feeling up on me and me dancing for them just so I could get money to pay one pissy-ass bill here and there. I was quitting ASAP, and I had one hundred thousand reasons to do so.

Jewel had been calling me from the moment that I had hit the Georgia State line. The bitch didn't give me a minute to breathe before she started hounding me about the money. She even had the nerve to tell me that Calico was pressing her hard and that she was having second thoughts about the plan. She was changing her mind and wanted the money back.

As far as I was concerned, that sounded like a personal problem. Hers, not mine. But I didn't tell her that. Instead, I just kept her at bay and told her that it was too late and that I had gone through with the original plan that she'd agreed to. I told her that she needed to relax until the money was flipped.

The truth of the matter was, Jewel wasn't ever getting shit from me, and I could have cared less if I'd ever spoken to her ass again. She was always the one on top, always the one shining, and finally it was my turn.

Two days after coming back to Atlanta, I had reached out to Touch. The nigga never called me back. I was always the one calling him and blowing up his phone, so I decided to keep calling until I got through to him, just so I could see where his head was at.

"Hello?"

"Touch, it's Sasha."

"Yeah, I know that, Sasha. What's up?"

I shook my head and sucked my teeth. "See, I knew it. So it was just about some pussy, right? So you just fuck and buck, Touch? Now you done hit it, you don't give a fuck."

Touch didn't say anything. Just like the punk ass he was, he started bitching up. As far as I was concerned, if it was just about pussy and he had gamed me, then it was all good. All I needed for him to do was to be a man about it and admit the shit. Hell, it wasn't the first time a nigga had gamed me for pussy.

"Sasha, listen, I'm in the hospital right now and I can't talk, but I'll call you back."

"Yeah, whateva," I said and then I hung up the phone.

I sat in silence for a while. I was pissed off. The longer I sat, the angier I got. I was so angry, I began crying tears of fury. All I wanted was to have shit going well in my life and to be in a committed relationship with someone that wanted to be with me for me, and not for any other false motives.

For the first time in weeks, I thought about Rick. Jewel and all my other fair-weather friends always had something negative to say about the father of my youngest child. But one thing that none of them ever understood was that Rick was the only person who ever accepted me for me and not for any other motives, and that was why I was so loyal and always felt indebted to him.

I'd met Rick years ago after I'd finished dancing one night. I was stopping at a local 7-Eleven to grab a soda when he and his boys were there buying up the place. We locked eyes across the aisle, while the other niggas were grabbing shit like it was The Last Supper.

I broke from my trance long enough to walk to the register. Before I could get the money for my soda, Rick told the dude to just add it to the rest of the shit he was buying. I thanked him and headed to my car. I didn't know he was behind me, until he I saw a hand reach for the car handle. I jumped back, and it was him.

"I just thought I'd open the door . . . and get your number," he said slyly.

I had to admit, it was a good move, but not that good to give him my number right away. So we talked outside of the 7-Eleven for a couple of minutes longer until his boys started harassing him to leave. I didn't give him my number, but he gave me his and made me promise to call. And we started talking on the phone every day after that.

It took me a whole year of knowing him before I told him I was a dancer. When I finally told him, he never condemned or judged me. Thinking back on it, I don't know why I would think he would be like these other cats out here. He was the only guy that I'd ever been with who didn't try to fuck me the same day, or within the first two weeks of knowing me. Nah, Rick was different. He waited six months before we fucked, and he was cool with that.

I don't know what I was thinking when I listened to Jewel and all of my dumb-ass friends. They didn't know what the hell they were talking about. Rick loved me, and I know that he did. Sure, he had hit some hard times and was going through a rough patch financially, but that was all good. I knew that he loved me and his son, and he'd supported me for years when he was getting money. Now it was my turn to return the favor.

So as my tears of anger subsided, they were quickly replaced by tears of joy that was mixed with regret.

I immediately dialed Rick's number. "Baby, I love you so much," I said to him when he picked up the phone.

"Sasha?"

"Yeah, baby, it's me," I said through my tears. I apologized to Rick for all the put-downs. "I'm just so stupid, always listening to my friends and shit. Now I realize they don't have my best interest at heart, but you do."

"You been drinking, Sasha?"

"Nooo, baby, I wasn't drinking. I'm serious. I was just sitting here thinking about how much I love you. I miss you and I want you to be with your son. I want the three of us to be together."

Rick started to say something, but I cut him off.

"Listen, baby, I did it. I did it, baby."

"You did what?"

"I did what I said I was gonna do. I came down here and I changed things around."

"Sasha, you're not making sense. What the hell are you talking about?"

"I got enough money to get us a nice two-bedroom

apartment, and I can pay the rent for one year up front, furnish the place, and get us a car. I can even give you the money to start your business. All I need you to do is just tell me that you'll come down to Atlanta and be with me and RJ."

I was desperately hoping that Rick would say yes. I mean, after all, I had done him dirty by walking out on him and turning my back on him.

"Whoa, I wasn't expecting a call from you like that," he said.

All this information I was giving to him at one time seemed to have him exhausted.

"Baby, just say yes."

Rick was silent for a moment, and then he spoke up. "You know I love you, right?"

"Yes, baby, and I know that you love RJ too."

"So if I come down there, it's just gonna be about me, you, and little man, right?"

"Of course. That's why I called you. Let's start over. Baby, I'm sitting on a pile of money right now, and we can start over and do it right."

Rick finally agreed to come down to Atlanta.

I was more excited than I had been in months. *Whoever said money can't buy you happiness definitely didn't know what the hell they were taking about.* I chuckled. All I knew was that I had my hands on some money, and I was happier than a pig in shit.

Chapter 25

"Forced into the Game"

Jewel

I felt like my world had turned upside down after speaking to Touch. He called me from jail. He had been charged with assault and battery on Ciara and her girl Monica. He didn't have a bond at the time, but his spirits were up. He'd already spoken to his attorney, and they were going up for a bond hearing the next day. He was sure he would get a bond. But shit wasn't looking so bright, as far as the charges. The judges in Virginia Beach had no mercy for convicted felons and definitely none for violent crimes.

It's funny how so much could happen in such a small amount of time. In three months alone, I'd met this new cat and was thinking about putting him on my team, only to start liking him. Before that shit could go any further, I get arrested and then attacked in my own home. Next, Touch comes to the rescue, tells me that he loves me, and we fuck. He goes and beats down his baby momma, and gets stabbed. Now he's in lock up.

To make matters worse, my gut feeling was telling me

that bitch had bucked on me with the money. At first she was giving me excuse after excuse, and finally it got to the point where she completely stopped answering her phone. Now, I'm out here in the streets alone with no Touch and without one hundred thousand dollars of Calico's money.

In a panic, I picked up my cell to give her one last try.

The automated recording said, "At the subscriber's request, the number that you are trying to reach has been disconnected . . ."

There was no need for me to listen any further. The message just confirmed my fear. The new-found gangstress in me wanted to take the first flight to Atlanta and search high and low for her ass and fuck her up on the spot, but my rational side forced me to sit down and think.

How the fuck am I gonna get out of this one? Come on, Jewel, this shit can't hold you down. I sat on a bar stool at my breakfast bar and sipped on a glass of White Zinfandel as I tried to put together the perfect plan. Unable to come up with anything, I gave up.

With a sudden loss of hope, I walked to my bedroom to try to get a little sleep. As I lay on my bed, I flipped through the channels on the television. I stopped on BET as I caught a glimpse of the letters TMF. *What are these niggas doing now?* I smiled as I thought back to the time I'd spent with them in New York. BET was covering a party TMF had thrown in Miami. The shit was crazy. They had white tigers in cages, searchlights in front of the club, and they arrived at the club by helicopter. *Damn, these niggas do it big!* I thought to myself as I sat and continued to watch.

All of a sudden it hit me. *Wait . . . TMF . . . that's the answer to my prayers.* I rushed to my desk and pulled out the copy of the contract I'd signed when I was in New York. There was a fifty thousand-dollar advance I would receive. It's not all of Calico's money, but it would be enough to help me get shit moving. *This is it, Jewel. Calico never believed that I was that bitch that can make things happen. If everything goes my way, I will show him why I'm not one to sleep on.*

After making a few phone calls and preparing myself to pull a few tricks if necessary, I was sure I could get that all in one lump sum, instead of the usual five disbursements. Then, after I had the cash in hand, I was sure I could convince Red, one of the head niggas of the TMF crew that showed a little added interest in me, to work with me on a good-ass price for some product. So there it was, shit was set. I had a plan. Now all I had to do was put that shit in motion.

I spent the next hour on the phone negotiating and trying to get everyone to agree to my terms. It wasn't easy, but in the end it was well worth it. I was able to convince the publishing company to agree to releasing the entire advance and wiring it directly to my checking account. I was even able talk Red into giving me a killer price, ten thousand dollars for each of those white girls. And on top of that, he was gonna throw double whatever I purchased. So I would have thirty keys.

So then came my next dilemma—getting rid of that shit. I knew Touch had my back, but shit wasn't looking too good for him. I hadn't heard from that nigga since he was arrested at the hospital and called me the next day from jail. So while I waited to hear from him, I decided to give my boy Diablo a call. From what I'd heard, he was doing it big in the *A*, and holding shit down in Virginia before the spot got hot. So he was known for doing his thing. After all, he was my ex-boyfriend, and I only fucked with dudes that get bread.

"Hello?" Diablo answered right away.

"Diablo?"

"What's up, baby girl?" he said, full of excitement.

"I need you to deal with some things for me."

"I thought your girl was coming down so you could grab some shit from me," Diablo said, oblivious to all the shit that had gone down between me and Sasha.

I updated him on the circus of events that had gone down between me and Sasha, and explained to him the new plan I had. He was ecstatic that he could get the white girl from me for eighteen grand a key. Diablo agreed to purchase fifteen keys right away, and the rest as soon as he moved those. I was sure Touch could handle the rest, but I agreed to Diablo's terms, until I knew what was up with Touch.

Now it was time for me to pull out the next thorn in my side, Calico. But as I was dialing his number, I thought about possibly killing two pesky birds with one large stone.

Calico picked up on the first ring, spewing disgust. That nigga didn't even greet me with a hello. "I hope you calling to say you got my muthafuckin' money, Jewel."

"Actually, I am . . . kinda."

"Kinda?"

I explained to Calico what went down with his money. "Look, I'm just gonna be straight-up and honest with you. Calico, I never tried to game you. I'm not the type to steal from anyone."

By then end of our conversation, I'd managed to turn shit around completely. I was the victim, and Sasha was the thieving bitch. Calico totally agreed with me. I was able to persuade him to forgive me and allow me the opportunity to pay him half in thirty days, and the other half thirty days after that, with interest added, of course.

Sure, in a matter of hours, I would have the money, and the right thing to do would have been to call Calico up and give him his money right away, but I needed some insurance. Shit, the world ain't fair. I ain't fuck him on that money; Sasha fucked me, and in turn, he got fucked. But I didn't know how Calico actually saw it or if he even cared. I knew that the easiest way to keep myself out of a toe tag was to keep him on a deadline date. Before I got off the phone, I commented again that I didn't fuck him over, Sasha did. I made that shit crystal clear to his ass, and he said that he would take care of it and then hung up.

I was instantly afraid for Sasha, but the emotion left just as quickly as it came. She tried to game me with my own rules. Now she had to pay.

Chapter 26

"Money over Bitches"

Calico

Jewel kept her word and finally hit my man Poppo off with all of my dough in thirty days, right before Thanksgiving. Originally she said that she would pay me half in thirty days and that she would give me the other half thirty days after that. So with her suddenly coming up with my money so quickly, I had instructed Poppo to make sure that he kept his eyes on both Jewel and Touch.

News came back to me that Touch, who had completely fallen off the radar for like a month and a half, had suddenly re-appeared back on the scene. I knew something was up. I didn't know exactly what, but I knew that what Poppo was telling me was true.

"Calico, on the real, Christmas ain't until next week, but I'm telling you Christmas done came early for this nigga Touch. The muthafucka got one of his homies driving him and Jewel around in a brand-new Maybach, and I heard they just purchased this big-ass crib out in the Heritage Park section in Virginia Beach. Jewel and Touch be pulling up to spots like they muthafuckin' Jay-Z and Beyoncé and shit. Yo, one of Touch's man is getting out and opening up the door for them like a gotdamn chauffeur."

I didn't say anything in response. All I did was chuckle into the phone.

"Last night Jewel was rocking a brand-new chinchilla coat. It's crazy. They got money from somewhere."

"Yeah, and that sounds like new money," I said.

"They the ones cutting our nuts and giving muthafuckas better prices than we can give 'em," Poppo said, confirming what I had already told him earlier.

I couldn't exactly prove the shit because when niggas like Touch get a new connect and that connect is giving them better prices, they horde that shit and guard that information with their life. And the fucked-up shit is that a muthafucka like Touch, who I was supplying with product, will turn around and start asking my ass if I need his product because the cost was so low.

When I reached out to Touch to see what was up and why he hadn't re-upped in a while with me, he gave me some bullshit excuse about shit being slow and him going to jail for a moment over some baby momma drama bullshit. Yet I had Poppo telling me him and Jewel was driving around, pushing brand-new half-a-million-dollar whips and shit.

"I'm gonna be out there for New Year's Eve. I had to lay low and stay off the radar for a minute, but I'm-a be back. We gotta get up with each other and break bread when I touch down," I said to Touch over the phone. I made sure not to make any mention of the new money I knew he was getting.

"Yeah, yeah, no doubt. We gonna get up," he said.

"Yo, so what's up with Jewel?"

"Jewel?"

"Yeah, what's up with her?"

"What do you mean?"

"Is she good?"

"Oh yeah, she good. Jewel is on some whole new get-money shit, and she getting it too. She ain't the same Jewel from a few months back."

"Oh yeah?" I replied on the other end of the phone with a half-smile. "So she doing it like that?"

"Yeah, she gettin that ghostwriting money. But you know Jewel is always gonna stay fly."

I took a sip of the gin and orange juice that I had been drinking. "Wow! Okay, so I guess I gotta break that bitch off some more dick." I started laughing into the phone. "For real, nigga, I don't how you ain't never hit that shit. She got the tightest and wettest pussy that I ever fucked. And I done had my share of pussy, you know what I mean?"

Touch didn't respond. I had to look at my phone to make sure we were still connected. I thought I had dropped the call or something.

"Touch, you there?"

"Yeah, yeah, I'm still here. So just hit me up when you get back in town."

"A'ight, fool." Just before I hung up I said, "Touch, keep it real with me—You fucking Jewel?"

"Me and Jewel go way back, you know that."

"But, I'm just saying, you sound like you caught feelings when I was talking about hitting that. And, I mean, a nigga will definitely back off and let you have my leftovers, you feel me?"

"Calico, this is the thing. Fuck this money that we getting, fuck breaking bread together and all that shit. If you gonna speak about Jewel, you make muthafuckin' sure that you don't speak disrespectful about her, a'ight."

I couldn't help but laugh at Touch and his clown ass. He was taking shit personal, like the little bitch he was.

"Oh, so that's your boo now?" I said. "It's all good. So, Encore, that's the spot for New Year's Eve?"

Touch didn't answer me.

"Keep your head up, fool," I said, still chumping his ass.

I could tell that Touch had a problem with me. I could sense the shit for some time, and I knew it had been brewing inside of him for a while and was about to come to a head. But it was all good, because now the nigga had cut into my money. I could give a fuck about Jewel 'cause, like a real nigga, I was always on some ol' money-over-bitches shit. But apparently Touch wasn't, and that was a prime example of why he wasn't built for this street shit like I was.

As far as I was concerned it was always about my money, and it will always be about my money. And that was why on New Year's Eve I was gonna see Touch. Yeah, I was definitely gonna see that nigga. He posed a threat to my money, and I had to do what I had to do in order to eliminate that threat.

Chapter 27

"I'm the King"

Touch

Thankfully for me my lawyer and the Commonwealth attorney had worked out a deal where I would plead guilty to the lowest degree assault charge possible and avoid doing any jail time. The judge would grant me time served for the month and a half that I had already spent in jail awaiting my trail, and I would also receive a sentence of five years probation.

I took that deal in a heartbeat. Yeah, I didn't want to deal with no probation and all that came with it, but at least I had my everyday freedom and wasn't locked behind no prison walls. Besides, without the barrier of prison walls, me and Jewel could focus on getting that money.

And leading up to New Year's Eve, getting money was exactly what me and Jewel did. With Jewel's TMF connect, all of my hustler dreams and ambition was being fulfilled. Me and Jewel were like the hood version of Kimora Lee and Russell Simmons. In a matter of a few short weeks, we were doing it up big and, that was only the tip of the iceberg.

I said to Jewel as I opened up the row of black garbage bags that contained one hundred and fifty thousand dollars in one-dollar bills. "You ain't never seen no shit like this before in your life, have you?"

"Niggas in them strip clubs be talking about making it rain, but I'm gonna make it rain up in Club Encore on New Year's Eve. As soon as that ball drops, I'm gonna have all this money drop from the ceiling and rain down on the crowd. Everybody's gonna know that ain't nobody doing it bigger than me and my girl." I scooped Jewel up and hoisted her into the air and kissed her.

"Yeah, but, baby, I don't know if that's a good thing, though."

"Why not?" I asked.

" 'Cause we don't need everybody knowing that we doing it up like that. This is all brand-new money, and we just started getting it like this. So I think we should keep a low profile, stack our money, and muthafuckas won't know shit, but we'll be rich as hell."

"Keep a low profile?" I laughed. "That shit went out the window when you leased that Maybach and purchased a seven-hundred-fifty-thousand-dollar house."

Jewel and I both started laughing.

"Yeah, you right about that. But, I'm just saying, from a jealousy standpoint, it's like when people see that kind of money just being wasted, then they'll know we getting money. And as soon as niggas get locked up and the detectives start pressing they ass for information, guess whose name is gonna come up even if we ain't have shit to do with anything? Yep, ours."

I knew that Jewel was right. Shit, everything I was doing was going against everything I believed in. I'd made promises after my first bid that I was gonna stay humble, well, as humble as possible, and play the game right this go-

'round. I knew a certain level of flossing always came at a price, and we definitely didn't need to give the feds a reason to start investigating us. And dropping one hundred and fifty thousand dollars in cash into a crowd was definitely a reason to get an investigation going. The authorities would want to know where in the hell were we getting all this money to just blow.

"Jewel, fuck it though. I'm-a keep it real with you. I'm gonna do that shit just to send a message to Calico. I want that nigga to know that, yeah, we getting money, and I that I got you on top of it, as icing on the cake."

"Touch, please. You got me, we got each other. Just fucking ignore Calico and his weak ass."

Jewel again was speaking logically and making sense, but I was determined to be hard-headed on this one. See, as far as I was concerned, yeah, it was always money over bitches, but I wanted to let Calico and the whole world know that not only did I have the money, but now I also had the top bitch. I wanted it all.

With my hands in the air like a king before his dynasty, I yelled to Jewel, "Like those TMF cats you so fond of say, 'The world is ours.' "

Chapter 28

"Never Satisfied"

Sasha

T hings had been going as well for me as I had ever envisioned. I had money in the bank, I wasn't waking up to no bullshit nine-to-five, nor was I shaking my ass in nobody's strip club. I had my apartment, I had my new furniture, I had my new Honda Accord, and most importantly, I had my man Rick with me.

So with things going well heading close to Christmas, I had decided to go to Bottoms Up just to chill and hang out and say what's up to some of the girls that I hadn't seen since I'd quit. When I walked into the club, I was greeted warmly by a bunch of the dancers. Everyone thought that I was coming back to work. It felt so good to just let them know that, nah, I was just there to have some drinks and be a spectator.

"What's up, baby girl?" some dude said to me as he came up behind me and put his hands over my eyes.

My first reaction was to think that it was one of the patrons who had recognized me from when I used to dance in there.

"Diablo! Hey, baby!" I said after he removed his hands from my eyes and I was able to turn around and see his face.

"What's up? Where the hell you been? You just vanished on everybody."

"I just been doing me," I explained.

Diablo ordered a drink, and the two of us drank at the bar and talked about a bunch of shit. And, of course, he was hitting on me the whole time, but I never gave in to any of his advances.

"So what's up with you and Jewel?"

"Fuck that bitch!"

"Damn! What's up? What happened between y'all two? I mean, she told me some shit, but I don't get it."

"Diablo, you don't need to get it. Like I said, fuck that bitch!"

"Damn! Okay, so I guess you ain't going to her and Touch's New Year's Eve party at Encore."

"Hell no!" I said with an attitude and a look of disgust on my face.

"They doing it real big up there in VA right now. I don't know, Sasha, you might wanna change your mind about not going." Diablo handed me his phone and told me to look at it.

I took hold of the phone and looked at a picture that Diablo had of him, Touch, and Jewel standing in front of a Maybach.

"Yeah, so?"

"Like I said, they doing it big up there. Jewel got the Maybach. She's killing 'em. That party is gonna be crazy."

"Can we please talk about something else? Anything but Jewel and Touch . . . please," I said to Diablo as I finished my drink.

"Okay, so I got another story for you." Diablo looked around from side to side as if he was being watched. "Word around town says that you offloaded some of the kingpin's money."

"What are you talking about now?" I said, trying to mask my sudden nervousness. *Where did he get this information from?*

"Well, about a couple of days after you came back into town, Jewel gave me a call. She told me how she couldn't get in touch with you, and asked me have I seen you? I told her, 'Nah,' but wondered what happened to that deal I was supposed to work wit' y'all. She told me that she had to find you to find out what happened. Fast forward to the present, and one of my mans an' dem is telling me that Calico is looking for you, and he wants you dead or alive. I just thought that you might wanna reach back out to your homegirl and see if she can try to extinguish the smoking gun that's about to come your way."

Diablo's words chilled me to the bone. With all my thoughts about getting over on Jewel, I forgot that she had that nigga Calico in her back pocket, and I didn't. Fear and anxiety was now showing on my face.

"You know what? I gotta go. I'll speak to you soon." I gave Diablo a kiss on the cheek and darted out the club.

Why, God? Why? Why me? I screamed in my head as I started up my car and peeled off, tears streaming down my face as I pressed my gas pedal to the floor. *I know that bitch worked out a deal with Calico*, I thought to myself.

I knew in my heart and in my mind that that couldn't be true. There was no way that Jewel could overcome the six-figure blow that I had dealt to her and recover so quickly and get a fucking Maybach without help from Calico or Touch. No way in hell. That bitch wasn't Superwoman, and her pussy wasn't all that. I know because I had the shit. *Fuck!* I thought to myself as I really began to hyperventilate.

As I pulled up to my apartment still in tears, I realized

that Jewel really must have thought that she was hot shit. As far as I knew, the bitch had never even tried to seriously track me down for the hundred thousand dollars. *Who the fuck does she think she is?*

I tried my best to gather my composure before exiting my car and going inside. I couldn't believe how much pain I was once again suddenly feeling because of Jewel. I was so tired of her always being one up on me, I just couldn't take it.

Yeah, I was gonna be at her and *her man's* little fucking party, but I wasn't gonna be there to party. I was gonna personally make sure that she felt some of the pain I was feeling at that moment. Yeah, my pain was more emotional than anything, but Jewel's pain was definitely gonna be physical.

Fuck that bitch!

Chapter 29

"Happy New Year"

Jewel

"Tonight is gonna be crazy," I said to Touch as I reviewed the checklist for the party setup.

Every celebrity from VA was on the guest list, and the VIP area would have a seafood buffet stacked with lobster tails and king crab and endless Armand de Brignac to wash that shit down. Each guest would receive a complimentary bottle of Rosé and a gift bag with party favors. There were dollar-sign ice sculptures, and dancers covered in nothing but body paint. They would be dancing in cages that hung from the ceiling throughout the club. And, of course, the ultimate one hundred fifty grand money-drop at midnight. I have to say Touch had really outdone himself this time.

Touch looked down at my brand-new five-thousand-dollar heels that had arrived just in time for the party. "Nah, these fucking custom-made Christian Louboutin heels are crazy."

I'd had a mold taken of my foot and had chosen the fabric myself, and had the shoes with a matching clutch custom-made for the night of the party. And my dress was tailor-made as well. This was one night I was confident that I wouldn't be duplicated.

"Look at us." I walked up to Touch and fell in his arms as I looked into his big brown eyes that I adored so much. "Who would have ever thought we would be here?"

"You're right." Touch laughed. "I should have fucked you a long time ago."

"Baby, I'm being serious. I mean, look at this." I grabbed a handful of money from the garbage bags and dumped them all over the bed.

"You did this, baby girl. You brought the shit to the table. I just rationed it out."

It wasn't until then that I realized what Touch was saying was true. I did make shit happen. When everything was fucked and I was alone, I made shit happen, using my money and my connection with TMF. For the first time I had some real gangtress credibility.

"Damn, I guess you're right. I never looked at it like that."

"I'm just glad that it's you that I have to build this with." Touch wrapped his arms around me and kissed me softly. "But I still say I should have fucked you a long time ago. Damn, a nigga was missing out. Time to play catch up." Touch pushed me on the bed playfully and rushed to take my clothes off, as if he had no time to waste.

"Stop playing, boy." I hopped on him and straddled my naked body over him. I whispered in his ear, "Your pussy ain't going nowhere."

"You sure?" Touch squirmed beneath me as he got undressed.

"I'm positive."

I could feel the head of his erect penis brush against my clit. That sensation alone made my juices flow. I moved my hips in a circular motion, forcing the head in and heightening the sensation even more.

Touch grabbed my hips, freezing them in position. "How do I know you won't give my pussy away?"

"Baby, I'm not," I said, eager to be released.

I wanted nothing more than to sit on his lap and have all of him inside of me. Each second he prolonged, the more I yearned for him. Unable to last a moment longer, I removed his hand and sat down on him, forcing his entire dick inside of me, and the next thirty minutes was spent in total bliss.

I opened my eyes as I panted, exhausted from a multiple orgasm triggered by the force of Touch's cum rushing inside of me at the peak of my orgasm. In front of me lay the love of my life, and all around him was money. Hell, the thought alone of fucking on a bed full of money was enough to get me wet all over again and go for round two, but time was ticking and we needed to prepare for our big night.

The next few hours were spent on hair and nails for me, and making sure everything was in order at the club for Touch. By ten o'clock were we getting dressed. Normally, we wouldn't be preparing so soon, but this night I wanted to be sure we were at the club by eleven. After all, the countdown was at eleven fifty-nine, and we had to be there for that.

Just as I'd planned, at eleven o'clock we were pulling up to the club. I was surprised to see such a huge crowd so early. The line was already wrapped around the building, and the valet parking was full of high-end cars.

When we pulled up, it was like the president and first lady had arrived. Security cleared the doorway, and they pulled out the red carpet. The driver ran around and opened the back door for Touch and me, and we paraded into the club as the onlookers stared.

The club was beautiful as we walked in. It was set up far better than I'd imagined.

Every known hustler and groupie was in the club, yelling

out to Touch as we headed to the VIP section toward the back of the club.

"Touch, what up, nigga."

"Yo, Trayvon."

Everything was about Touch. He was the big man in town. As we walked through, I received dirty looks from bitches cutting their eyes and pointing and whispering, while dudes looked like they wanted to kidnap me. Touch was the town savior, while I was the city's most hated.

I held in my irritation as I held my man's hand tight as we walked through the club. Never would I let anyone see me weak.

Once we got to the back, I noticed a big chair that resembled a throne.

As soon as Touch walked up, the club owner said, "Take your seat, homeboy."

Touch dapped him up. "Nigga, you crazy as hell."

"I had to show love. Ain't nobody ever did it big like this in the club yet, so I had them bring this chair in for you. This is your seat for the night."

"A'ight, a'ight." Touch got comfortable as he sat at his throne.

Just then two naked-ass bodypainted bitches came over. They kneeled before Touch and asked, "What can we get for you?"

Touch looked at the club owner, who still stood beside him. "The bitches too?"

"You the king tonight, homie."

"Oh, this is just too much." I walked away to get a glass of champagne from the fountain.

Touch met me at the champagne fountain moments later. "You a'ight, baby?" he asked.

"I'm good. Don't worry about me. It's all about you tonight. Just do you, king," I said sarcastically before attempting to walk away.

Touch grabbed my arm. "Jewel, don't do this tonight, please."

He was right. I didn't want to let the people see us weak. Regardless of what, we needed to put our best foot forward and show them that our empire was strong.

"Okay, no problem." I put on a plastic smile, kissed him on the cheek, and followed his royal highness to his throne.

As the night went on and I downed glasses of champagne, any insecurities I had earlier in the night were gone. Touch and I laughed and danced. With two minutes left until midnight, I caught a glimpse of Sasha. She was talking to the security at the entrance of VIP. My first instinct was to rush over there and beat that bitch's ass. But again that night I had to put my best foot forward. Besides, security was tight, and I was sure there was no way her ass would get past them.

As Touch rushed to grab two bottles of Armand de Brignac, the deejay said, "One minute."

The crowd grew anxious as we all awaited the countdown. With thirty seconds left until midnight, I glanced at the VIP entrance and noticed Sasha was no longer there. *I knew that dirty bitch wouldn't get through.*

Touch handed me my bottle. He tapped me and nodded his head in the direction of the crowd, signaling me to look at someone.

As I pulled the wrapper off, preparing to pop the top, I noticed Calico in the VIP area.

We all counted down in unison, "Ten, nine, eight . . . zero."

Everyone shouted, "Happy New Year!" and bottles began to pop. Everything around me was chaotic. The crowd was going crazy as the money dropped from the ceiling. It sounded like a combination of fireworks and gunshots as the bottles and balloons popped uncontrollably.

"Happy New Year, baby." Touch kissed me passionately.

"Look at this shit. Ain't nobody ever did it this big." Touch then stood up on the seat of the throne. He yelled, "The world is mine!" and began to pour champagne on all those around him.

I shook my head as I watched. His boys encouraged him, handing him bottle after bottle, and the soaking wet groupies surrounded him. The bodypainted bitches were now virtually naked because the champagne had begun to rinse the paint away. The more I watched, the angrier I got. I'd finally had enough.

I called out to Touch. *This world is fucking mine. I made this shit happen. I'm the queen of this dynasty. I built the fucking empire.*

Just then I heard a gunshot. In a state of panic, I looked up at Touch, and we locked eyes. Then, in what seemed like a split second later, I felt a striking pain in my head. I collapsed to the floor, and within moments, I could hear no noise. Everything was still and eventually went black.

The End

California Connection 2

Chapter 1

"Mad New Year"

Sasha

My blood was boiling as I watched Jewel and Touch step out their Maybach and onto the red carpet like they were the fucking king and queen of England. All around them stood crowds of people calling and reaching out to them like the paparazzi, and others, like peasants, just stood in awe, wishing they could have one moment in their shoes. No matter which crowd you belonged, you still went unnoticed by the royal couple as security guards forced people out of their way to open a clear path for them to enter the club. Realizing I was amongst this crowd of peasants and paparazzi, I inched my way toward the front of the line that wrapped around the building.

I called out to one of the bouncers that guarded the front door of the club and gave him my most seductive look, "Excuse me, sweetie," but this dude just glanced at me then turned his head.

Muthafucka. I couldn't believe this guy.

Still determined to get in the club, I dug into my purse, bypassing my hand-sized .22 caliber, and pulled out a hundred-dollar bill, knowing that money talks. This time I didn't even bother calling out to him, I just walked toward the entrance.

The bouncer said, "This is VIP, ma'am. Are you on the list?"

"Yes, I am," I said, sliding the money in his hand. Moments later, I was walking through the door, no search and no hassle.

I couldn't believe the sight before me. Jewel and Touch was really on some celebrity shit. They had definitely taken things to the next level in VA. *Well, at least Jewel would have a chance to have a hell of a farewell party.*

I watched the time as I made my way toward the VIP area. It was eleven thirty. I had thirty minutes to make it to the back, where Touch and Jewel partied. I wanted to be sure I was there to bring Jewel's New Year in with a bang.

I stopped at the bar and purchased a bottle of Ace of Spades. I needed all the props I could get, to look like I belonged in the VIP area. I knew it would be even harder getting past this security guard. Niggas passed a hundred dollars all night to get in the VIP, so I knew that may not fly this go-'round.

After fighting a crowd of groupies, I finally made it to the entrance of the VIP. The time was now five to midnight. I needed to get in VIP, and fast.

"Excuse me, hon," I said to the security guard to get his attention.

"Malibu?" He called me by my dance name, causing me to take a closer look at him.

This must be my lucky day. This gotta be a sign that the New Year is gonna be my year. I let out a sigh of relief, realizing this guy was a bouncer at a club I used to dance at.

I put on my best game. "Hey, boo. I'm trying to get back there and celebrate with my girl Jewel. I just flew in from Atlanta, and I want to surprise her. I just bought this bottle so we can pop it and bring in the New Year together."

The security stepped back, unhooked the velvet rope, and allowed me through. As I headed toward the back, the countdown to midnight began. I spotted Jewel and prepared to give her that long-awaited gift as I rushed in her direction.

As the countdown ended, the crowd went wild as everyone yelled, "Happy New Year!"

I watched as Touch stood on his throne and sprayed champagne over a crowd of groupies. No one even noticed me standing directly behind Jewel. With fire in my eyes, I took a deep breath then delivered.

Bam! One to the back of her head and she was down.